God Breath

Through Natl

٢٥٤

God Breathes His Dreams
Through Nathaniel Cadwallader

Charlotte Fairbairn

review

First published in 2002
by REVIEW

An imprint of Headline Book Publishing

10 9 8 7 6 5 4 3 2 1

ISBN 0 7553 0182 X

Typeset in Minion by Palimpsest Book Production Limited,
Polmont, Stirlingshire
Printed and bound in Great Britain by
Clays Ltd, St Ives plc

Headline Book Publishing
A division of Hodder Headline
338 Euston Road
London NW1 3BH

www.reviewbooks.co.uk
www.hodderheadline.com

for Grandmama

Acknowledgments and thanks:

to Antonia B, Naomi C, Sophie C, Robert N and Dido S for patiently reading through early drafts;

to happy times at Goursac;

to Kate, to Copps Hill Farm, to all those blissful Virginian days;

to Helen Corner for her meticulous professionalism;

to Simon Trewin for daring to run with his passion;

to Mary-Anne Harrington for daring to run with hers;

to EMF and GRP for their unstinting support throughout.

Part One

One

He is poised against the background of an auburn sky. Poised on the edge of a craggy path, at the foot of a hill, at the top of another, with a grand sweep of rock and fell and moorland barren stretching out before him. Silhouette of a man on his horse, cut out against the reds and the ambers of a brilliant dusk. All around, the fells are clad with heather, reedy grass. It is bare here, tussocky there, the dark earth dotted with clumps of arid green. Sheep and goats pick at the ground. Plovers dart in the grass, a buzzard swoops on the dying currents of the day.

Astride his horse and he surveys the landscape that drops below: to the west, the wide purple blanket of the sea; to the north, the hills; to the south and east, the comforting menace of the forest; and far below, beneath the moor, encircled by sea and hills, forest and fell, a triangle of soft-bottomed, lime-green humps. And enfolded in this tiny oasis, a cluster of farms and houses, low-slung, mean-windowed, shy of the winds. There is beauty here, beauty and softness, remoteness. And yet there is also something cruel, a hardness – the hardness of a small place in a small time with few people and some bleak winds.

*   *   *

In the far distance, as the rocks climb up again to meet the sky, you make out two figures. A girl, perhaps, tall, maybe young, maybe not so young, you cannot tell. She wears a shawl, she carries a stick, she minds some sheep, some goats. And behind her, walking slowly, a man. And he is old, you are sure of that, because he stoops a little, because his hat appears stuffed down upon his head, because he looks as if he is shuffling, dragging his feet as he makes his way down the hill towards her.

Though you cannot be sure, it seems that the man gives the girl a fright. She jumps. He reaches out to hold her and she jumps again. He pulls at her, this time not missing. You cannot hear what is said but surely there are words because, from as far away as you are, you feel that this is an ugly encounter.

Soon the tussle appears more violent. You see the girl, only now her arms are flailing and then she is lying with her back pressed against one of the stone walls that reach out in short stretches, here and there across the fell. Her shawl is on the ground. Her stick is broken in two. The man is pressing himself down upon her and you strain to hear a sound, to make out a scream or a cry or a prayer for help but the wind is sharp and the air is filled only with salt and cold and raw.

You want to go to her aid. You want to hurtle down the scree and the rock, the fell and the bumps and up the other side and you want to take this man and hurl him to the floor. You want to take the broken stick and poke his eyes out, break the splinters over his back, make him see somehow that what he is doing is what should never be done. You see the girl's arms as they thrash beneath him. You see her hair as it lies strewn across the top stones of the wall. You see the rise and fall of the old man's trousers and deep down you are enraged but you know that you will never get there – it is too far, it is too late, you are no one.

At last, the wind abates and you hear a sound, a long scream and it rends the air of the day as it fades through the valley. The buzzard has made his catch, the young rabbit puts up its frail, useless struggle. You see the old man stand up now. He is drawing up his trousers, fiddling with his buttons, stuffing his hat again down upon his head. He does not turn back to look at the girl but he sets off back down the path, down towards the village, and you see her and even from here you can see she is broken, that her shoulders are slumped, that her neck is slumped, that all the strength that she might ever have had has abandoned her.

For what seems like an age, she lies there and you begin to wonder, maybe she is unconscious, maybe worse and so you start to make your way, kick your horse beneath you, trip down the mountain and it is a perilous journey and a slow one because this is the steep side and you are not sure, maybe you will have to leave your horse but at last you reach her and you jump down and you see where the ground has been rubbed by knees that were going back and forth, back and forth.

Her eyes are not shut, only glazed. Her life is not gone, she does not seem unconscious, only she is numb and she does not acknowledge him and she does not smile when he lifts her up and she does not soften when he wraps her in his grip. Up close, he sees she is after all quite young – maybe twenty. He sees the rips in her dress and the scratches on her face and hands and arms, and the bruises. He sees marks left from tears that dried in terror.

He goes down the path. He does not know where he is going but he follows the path and soon he comes to a shed – looks like a shearing shed – and he lays her down on a heap of hay that lies in the corner and he makes her as comfortable as time and circumstance allow. And then he leaves because he does not belong here, this is not his business, he is no one.

As evening comes, the growling sea, the scavenging sheep graze on, growl on.

.

The girl sits. Her long fingers are blue at the tips. Her thighs are growing lined where the hay presses hard into her flesh. Her hair, dishevelled, lifts in the wind that seems to be blowing up this October evening. Look in her eyes and you see there is no life. Look at the state of her dress and you know there is no life for surely no girl would sit here like this, with her clothes in such a state.

Now it is growing late. Other villagers, they begin to come down off the fell. The men. They have been mending a wall on one of the top paddocks, mending it before the storms blow in and the stones roll down the side of the mountain. Tom Sebley out in front. He is whistling, tapping the ground with his stick. Alfred Clothier, Bertie Hotblack, the men Jones, Jessop and Cartwright, Duddon Sheepshanks and Reilly MacReilly, the boys Penhaligon, Shiny Blackford. At the back, Lysander Merritt, struggling a bit because his hips are stiff and his bones are tired and nothing works as it should.

Each of these men walks past the shearing shed. Tom whistles on – he is cheerful because a night in the tavern is in prospect. The boys Penhaligon too are noisy because when have you ever seen them otherwise and, besides, Duddon and Reilly are there to egg them on. Alfred Clothier, in a hurry because Bethan will have his supper ready, because the children will be playing up and she'll be in a temper and it'll be all the worse for him. Shiny Blackford, cheerful also because Shiny is always cheerful, because Shiny is looking forward to an evening in her bothy, with her and her warm bread and her sweet smile.

Were her eyes working as they should, Megan would see the troop of shadows as it marches past. Were her ears not filled with her own wails of anguish, she would hear them come and she would hear them go and with her voice, if only she could summon up some strength, she could shout out Stop-come-back, stop-come-back!

But neither of these things happens, no one sees the girl, no one stops to pick her up or carry her home or wipe her forehead or ask her what has happened because time is moving on and the clouds are joining as one and soon the place is engulfed in dark and everything is silent – except in the tavern where all is noise and cheer, where Tom's voice rings out above the hum and everyone laughs in appreciation of his fine words.

And then it is up to Shiny because Shiny goes to her bothy and he expects the smell of warm bread but he knocks on the door and all that answers him is the quiet of an empty house. And Shiny, who has loved Megan for as long as he can remember, Shiny senses at once that something is wrong. It is growing late now, the shadow – blue and grey – of the church has long ago crept over Megan's bothy. It is two hours, three, since Daisy should have trotted into view leading the others, Megan behind. Shiny steps down into her bothy but he knows she is not there. He calls out Megan, Megan but he does not wait because he is certain there will be no reply. A wind is getting up, a sharp wind, whistling through the tops of the trees around the church, but Shiny does not listen because his heart is beginning to thump a little harder and his mind fills with apprehension, she could have fallen she could be injured she could have cried out and not been heard she could be sitting at the bottom of an empty shaft she could be in a faint she could be all alone she could be so, so afraid, she could be dead . . .

He climbs up out of the steep low doorway into the thickening darkness, up into the churchyard, up beyond the church, along the lane, up and out on the open track towards the fells where the sheep and goats are grazed. On and on and on and Shiny never seems to get there. On and on and round and round his fears. Then he comes to the shearing shed – Shiny Blackford is heading for the lower fell, searching for his friend, his girl, and on his way he comes by the shearing shed and he would not go inside but that he sees Daisy there, why he's sure that's Megan's favourite goat, Daisy.

Shiny steps off the track just to make sure that he's not mistaken, just to make sure that Megan is not sitting there all alone with the life and the smile and the joy knocked clean out of her. But she *is* there, she is sitting there, unsmiling, joyless, lifeless, Megan Capity, on a heap of hay. Why, what on earth . . . says Shiny but Megan does not even look up when he comes. She does not even look up when her old friend Shiny Blackford comes and finds her like this.

Shiny does not see the stranger on the far side of the fell – he is too intent – and he goes to her, rushes towards her, picks her up in his tiny ramrod arms and he carries her back along the track, down the hill, under the shadow of the tall, dark church, back down through the open door and into the nest of her parlour. Gently, he sits her in her oak-dark rocker. Tenderly, he offers her a morsel of yesterday's bread, holds a glass of water to her cracking lips. But Megan will not touch the water, will not eat, does not stir. She does not speak, does not move, does not focus her grey-dead eyes.

Those days and weeks that follow are a grave source of worry to Shiny Blackford. From dawn to dusk, Megan sits wordless, sightless. Some few drops of water drizzled on to her chin keep her from fading altogether and Shiny barely leaves her side. Her hair turns white. You look at her hands and they are shrivelled and wrinkled like those of an old washerwoman. You look at her back, at the stance of her and she is hunched, drooped like someone five times her age.

Visitors come – Bessie Hotblack, Bethan Clothier. They click their tongues, take her limp hand in theirs, wonder secretly what can have happened. But they can offer no true help and Shiny is beside himself. What will he do? How will he bring his Megan back from this twilight world? Brutally, unexpectedly, the innocence and levity of their times together have been destroyed. Just look at her – her hair is white and her tongue is cold from its weeks of idleness and her clothes, those same ones that she wore on that day when he found her in the shearing shed, they grow long and baggy around her wilting form.

Lord Almighty, says Shiny, Lord Almighty, he cries. What can I do, what can I do?

One evening, when all seems nearly lost, Shiny leaves the bothy in despair. He cannot bear any longer to watch his friend disappear before his eyes. He goes for a walk, as they used to when they were children. Shiny does not wish to walk the fields but he takes the winding path, the one that leads through the forest, the one that leads to the sky and the birds and the secret magical waters of the swanny-pool.

When he reaches the margin, Shiny kneels. He dips his hands in the water, brings them up to his forehead, wipes them deep and slow over his exhausted eyes.

Today, it is quiet here. Today, the light dances on the water, tilts in its stillness and Shiny shares these moments only with the coots and the moorhens, only with the trees and the man in the distance who watches him unseen. Shiny says to himself I will bring her here. He says I will bring her here for here is where she will mend her broken spirit.

Shiny goes to one of the farmers and buys a rickety willow cart. He goes to another and buys a black donkey colt. He comes to the bothy and Megan, who is barely conscious now, through the fog of her pain and her shock, she hears an unfamiliar noise – sound of geese, sound of a crying man? – and then she feels Shiny's arms as he lifts her up once more, as he carries her into the cart, as he holds her straight while he drives up the track to the swanny-pool.

Imagine you are in a long, dark tunnel, that your eyes have been sightless and your ears without sound and your hands and feet and nerves just dead, heavy and dead. Thus you are for many weeks, long and murky weeks – and then suddenly, in front of you, there is a mirror, one that goes from the sky to the floor, a mirror that is made from water and jewels. Suddenly you open your eyes and you look into the mirror and you see before you something you know well, something with which you are familiar, with which you feel warm and at ease. Your eyes run the length of this form, top to bottom, side to side, friendly with all that you have known and then they stop. There is a rush of blood to your head, your heart, for you have seen, in the translucence of this magic mirror, you have seen not only that your body

10

has returned to you from a long, a desperate journey. You have seen that you bear within your fragile form the tiny sleeping kernel of a child.

Megan looks through the dripping veils of cobwebs that dance on the trees that dip their toes in the waters of the swanny-pool. She looks at the rippling mirror that stretches out before her. She sees her belly, she sees the child, she feels the trickling of sensation as it creeps back into her mind. She sees Shiny standing by her, awe-struck, hopeful, waiting, his mouth half opening as though he would say the words he is praying she will say herself. She sees the Old Man and the way his skin hangs from his chest like strips of old cloth. She sees his eyes, the way they cloud over – just briefly, just for a second or two, just enough to give her something she had never asked for, something she was far too young to have.

She could never want this child. How could she? She could never look at him as though he had been all her heart was ever set on. She could never believe in her heart that this was for the best. She could never pick him up and hold him high above her head and laugh, like you do, laugh because there are songs in your veins and sun in your hair. She could never turn round and look at Shiny and smile because it was his, it was theirs, they had made it together one day, one beautiful sunlit afternoon.

She looks into the mirror of the swanny-pool and she sees guilt, only guilt. Sensation has returned to her mind and Megan feels the aching impact of all those endless minutes pressed up against the dry-stone wall. Overnight, she has aged. Overnight, she has been forced to shed her childhood, to rearrange her hopes. It is guilt because she did not stop him. It is guilt because she could not prevent herself for just one eye-blink moment from moaning, from letting out a sigh which might have said to the Old Man – though surely God it never should have – it might have said that she had taken part in something almost good. It is guilt because here, now, growing beneath her dress is someone she will never truly love.

Shiny watches as Megan slowly comes back to life. He wills her hair to shed its brittle white, to resume the old deep chestnut he has known so long. He wills her back to straighten, her tongue to loosen, her legs to regain their strength. He watches as her eyes start to move in recognition of where she is, who she is. He sees her lips move and he feels sure it is a smile, a timid smile that drifts on to the corner of her mouth. She turns, she sees him, it must be that she smiles.

But Shiny cannot see inside of her. He cannot see that she has gone, that the girl who held his hand through the long sun-balmed carnival of their childhood has disappeared.

October turns to November, autumn to the early grip of winter and the rains pour down as they have never done before. Rain, rain and the streets are filled with water and the fields are thick with mud and you cannot step into your parlour but your feet are drenched and your knees are soaked and the hem of your dress becomes heavy with the damp.

Then come the winds and they are fierce, fiercer than they have ever been. Step into the tavern on these winter nights and all you hear – the only words that can be deciphered above the hum and thrum – speak of the rain and the winds, of water, water, water, flooding, broken-soaking-drenched-and-drowning, worst bloody winter we ever had make no mistake.

Megan struggles to keep the water at bay. Shiny does not come, Megan has pushed him away because she cannot bear to see his pleading eyes, because she cannot bear a man to be close to her, because she is ashamed and bruised and unable to placate the terrible gnawings of her guilt. Yet alone, she cannot match the strength of this vehement weather. The floorboards in her gleaming parlour lose their sheen. One by one, her shutters fall from their hinges, her windows crack and leak, her doors rot. Megan bends down to lay a block of wood across her door but now her belly is too large and she can barely reach. Water seeps in. Megan wishes that she were not so heavy, that this bloody winter would come to an end. She worries for Daisy and her flock of sheep. She tries in vain to keep her cottage clean, she retires at night to the safety of her upstairs bedroom and prays that soon her child will come, that soon the Good Lord will lose his anger, that the rains will go and the winds will go and her child will come.

Years later, when Megan is old and blind, when she sits all day in her chair, turning it as the sun turns round the valley so that she can feel the warm on her eyes, she remembers those days when she waited, waited, waited for her son Donald to arrive. March turned to April, April to May but still there was no sign of spring. Still the rains dragged on and the snow blew in and the winds kept whipping across the limp brown prairie that had been left by all this water. Megan grew and grew, her legs were weary, her back screamed at the end of every day. So wet it was, she remembered, that there were no daffodils – for the bulbs rotted in the ground, along with the snowdrops, the crocuses, the bluebells. And all the blossom that there should have been – on the hawthorns, on the horse chestnuts – all the blossom seemed to stay within its cups, as though God were angry, as though God did not want the people of the valley to sip on the pleasures of a brand-new year. The broom, the gorse, the fruit trees – they all hid within themselves; the birds did not sing, there was no sign, none at all that the seasons were there, were progressing as they should. And all the while, Megan grew and the fields stayed brown and the stock went hungry for want of grass.

Now it is June, still deep winter and Megan can scarcely move. Why should they be so punished? Why must she wait so? How will they go on like this when the sheep have nothing to eat, when the cattle pine and the sward has gone and all that there is on the ground where grass should be are roots and stones and mud? Megan tries to mend the shutters, she tries to wax the floors, she struggles to keep the demons of *that day* at bay while she waits for her time. She runs her hand around the vast dome of her belly and she tries to think kind thoughts, good thoughts. She tries to will some love, real maternal instant doting love down her fingers, through the wall of its cocoon. She wonders what it will be like, how it will be to be a mother, to hold in the bend of her arms another being like her. She wonders how she will create the illusion that says this child is wanted, this child is needed. Sometimes she says to herself well maybe I did ask him, maybe I did bring him to me with my eyes or my pinny or the way my hair was blowing a bit. She says well maybe I should go to him and I should show him what he has done – at least that. She never knew what innocence was before. She never knew just what she had, how simple it was. She never knew how good Shiny was, how kind. She never saw that the valley was so small, that the people were so small, that life could be so cruel, that she could possibly feel so low, so godforsaken god-abandoned low.

And then, just when it seems that she can wait no longer, when it seems that her mind and her body are all for exploding, when it seems that the stock are on the verge of starvation and the valley is stretched to breaking-point, Megan takes to her bed and she has a dream. She dreams that twenty feet of snow land in a smothering blanket about the valley. Everyone – Shiny, Alfred Clothier, Bethan Clothier, Lysander Merritt, the Hotblacks, Mary Jessop, Archie Jessop, Tom Sebley, Reilly MacReilly and Duddon Sheepshanks – wakes in the morning and finds that they cannot see out of their windows, that their doors are jammed and the walls of their houses are freezing cold to the touch. The great west door of the church is filled to its height with snow, the windows are half-blocked with snow, the headstones in the shadowy graveyard are all buried. On this day, Megan's village is little more than a forest of chimneypots and weather vanes.

Megan dreams that she is the only one awake on this night. She dreams that in her vastness, in her impatience, in her thirsting hunger to deliver this wretched child of hers, she lies upstairs in her bed but does not sleep. From her upstairs window, she watches as flakes the size of handkerchiefs pile one upon one, another upon another in a giddying, relentless kaleidoscope.

Megan dreams that throughout the night, she lies and watches until at last she can bear it no longer. In spite of her girth and her ungainliness, she is roused to go outside and explore the incredible bleached landscape that is rising around her. But first she must scrape her way out of the half-buried cottage so she opens the door, crouches low as she can upon her haunches and she sets to digging a channel through the snow that is already higher than the doorframe itself. *Pfssh!* but it is cold and her fingers are numb and her hands are raw. Megan digs, she digs and digs yet all the while she has her eyes up and her head high for God is magnanimous in his anger and now that it is dawn, he has stopped the snow and is sending instead an eclipse, colours as dark and lowering as they are many-splendoured. At last, at last, Megan can see the top of her tunnel and she heaves and squeezes her bulk through the nose of it and she pulls herself high, high into a landscape that is far beyond the fantasy of dreams.

There is a soft wind and it is blowing so the snow is swirling lightly up against the walls and the buildings and you are standing or you are walking in a white mist with the sky as clear as you will ever see it. The valley is as you have never seen it before, will never see it again, and you start to walk in the place that you have known since you were a child, start to walk about the village and the valley, only you are taller than you have ever been before and the sky is closer and the clouds are gone and God is smiling down the drop of your dress, breathing the warm of a fresh smile and a new day in the hair of you, in the arms of you, in the way that you run and the way that you feel and all you can do is keep running, keep laughing, keep your arms outstretched and your hair hanging loose down the ridge of your back.

You might walk into something and think oh damnation, if I haven't bumped into a gatepost – but it's no such thing, it's a chimneypot or the church weather vane or the top of a tree. It sets your eyes blinking and your breath gasping and your heart racing. There is a cool, thick blanket of snow that

16

lies in soft bumps over the houses and the church and the trees – it is just as if you had taken a great rug of your best, your whitest, largest ewe fleece and lain it over the top of everyone while they slept.

There is a shimmer in the air, magical darts of colour that trail and creep across the sunburnt sky. There is a blueness that dazzles you, a purple glinting beauty and you smell the starkness and you feel the coldness and you hear the clean, wisping echoes of the birds and the animals who are hurtling from here to there, who are calling, who cannot place themselves in a landscape where everything is white. You are blinded, bedazzled. Your heart, your eyes, your mind are in a whirl, your legs are jelly, you fall to the floor and you pray, not knowing what to say but praying just the same, saying anything that comes into your head, anything at all because it is all just so beautiful, so astonishing and so, so beautiful. And you are lying outstretched upon the frosted counterpane, looking up at the spattered palette which God has hurled across the canvas of his sky when you feel the pain, the wide shafting pain that can only mean one thing – that can only mean that your child is coming at long, long last.

What will you do, who will you call, how will you manage? And what if it comes and you are both lying together on the cold white floor and you cannot get up and make the child warm and you cannot make him clean, what then, what then? And what if the child gets stuck, if his legs tie in knots and his head just will not budge and there is no one there to ease him out? Megan had not expected this. She had not expected to be giving birth alone on a cold white floor with no one for company, no eyes to look upon her but the glaring eyes of a bleached and hostile sky.

17

Then you sink down into a well that seems to be without end – gone the spattered palette, gone the purple glinting beauty. Now you are calm and dark and slow and though you may not wish it so, your child is coming now, coming fast.

In your dream, a man with broad shoulders sitting astride a tall, conker-brown stallion rides suddenly into the range of your belladonna eyes. He sees you prostrate upon the cold white floor and he slips down from his stallion and wraps his woollen cloak about your numbing body. You are chilled, lost in your well and you do not truly see this man, cannot decipher his face. Is he old, is he young, is he dark, is he fair, is he a man, a boy, a god? You cannot tell but you lie within the nurture of his cloak and, like it or not, you pass into his unknown hands the glistening bundle that is your new-born son.

In your dream, a man with broad shoulders rides suddenly into your view and he rescues you and your son from a certain death. His cloak is warm, his arms are kind, his grip is safe and he plies your infant son with care, solicitude, the tenderness of a lover. In your dream, you are lifted, you and your son, from the cold white floor, across the purple glinting landscape, back past the chimneypots and weather vanes, back down the hand-carved tunnel, down into the cottage that lies in the lee of the church, along the mud-soaked floorboards of the parlour, along and up the stairs and into the warmth and familiarity of your upstairs bed. In your dream, this man does not speak to you, does not say who he is nor where he is from but places you and your son beneath the covers of your bed and turns on his heel just as quietly, just as darkly as he came.

And in your dream, you wake up and you look out of

your upstairs window and you see that spring and summer and the flowers and the birds, they have all come at once – at last, at last! And what a spring! Days of yellow, days so yellow that the houses, the trees, the sky are golden, glowing. Everywhere you look is tinged with the light from the primroses, the celandines, the daffodils and buttercups and dandelions who surely must have planned it, surely. Days of birdsong. The trees echo, ring out for joy and the tambourines and clarinets, the flutes and oboes wake you, blackbirds, thrushes, linnets, finches, singing as you have never heard them sing before. Days of blossom, days when you look out – you are standing high and the whole of the valley lies out before you – and all you can see are the hawthorns and the fruit trees, the horse chestnuts and the hedgerows garlanded in white, shell-fragile flowers. The valley is shawled in white, swathed like a babe, a snow queen, like a virgin bride.

And as you bathe in the glow of all this beauty, all this joy and yellow and carefree heart-lift singing, you turn in your duck-feathered bed and you look and you see that beside you lies a son. And you try to remember the dark, strange man who rode by upon his stallion – you try to remember his face, to recall whether or not you said thank you Lord, Thank You for saving me, for delivering my son, for saving us both from the cold and the white and the dawn.

But you cannot remember – in your dream, you cannot remember.

Then the days come by, the snow gone, the spattered palette no longer, the sheep lambed and the grass green and the valley filled with the sounds of summer and you venture out of your house, now that your son is born, now that you are a mother and he is your boy and you ask the people did you see the snow, did you see the eclipse, did you see the man upon the conker-brown stallion who came by and delivered my son?

And, in your dream, though the people do not know the answers, though the people did not see the snow nor the sky nor the man nor the horse nor the full sweep of God's power – for they were all asleep in their beds – the mountains whisper to you and the trees whisper to you and the birds and the bees and even Daisy and the lambs and the sheep and the deer that live in the spinney all whisper to you that his name was Nathaniel Cadwallader, that Nathaniel Cadwallader has come to this valley to breathe the dreams of God.

Two

When Tom Sebley was a child, the others were afraid of him. He was not one of them. Perhaps it was his age – so much younger than the elders, so much older than the children. Perhaps it was the way he walked, with his hands braced on the edge of his hips – or the grin, that tiny grin that lurked on the corners of his creeping mouth. Perhaps it was his height or his smell or his voice. With Tom Sebley, you never knew. You could share a cup of tea with Tom Sebley but you would not know whether he was with you or against you.

And you could watch him, watch the games he played with the younger ones, the way he liked to draw them around him, the way he relished his height against their shortness, his age against their youth. You could see he was a nettle among dandelions and the small boys – the Reillys and the Duddons and those boys Penhaligon – would move as one, would laugh as one, would jump or fight or shout or run as one, just like Tom Sebley told them. They would all say yes, Tom, no, Tom. They would all laugh in a raucous crowded puff of laughing which meant nothing.

And then with the elders it was the same and you could see it was the same. How he made friends with the Old Man and Lysander Merritt and especially with Father Standage. How he sidled up to them as they were having a drink, how he slapped them on the back, roared with laughter – too loud! – at anything they said. How he always used their first names, how he always remembered their problems, every last grievance, how he stored it all away like a rat stowing cheese. How he would smile sometimes when he thought no one was looking and you knew it was because he had discovered a secret. How he always had opinions – so many! – how they always fitted in somehow with everyone else's opinions, how he was always happier with the weak ones, how he always stayed sober enough to remember, how he always looked at the likes of Shiny and Megan as though they were the dirt beneath his feet.

From his youth to his old age, he held them. He held their minds, their wits, their eyes. He held their strength and in the palm of his hand, in the softness of his weaving fingers, he held their weakness. With Tom, they were stronger, braver, better. With Tom, they would do things they might not otherwise dare to do. With Tom Sebley, the village was filled with strong people, a tribe, some droplets that became a cloud.

He was careful, too, Tom Sebley. He did not drink or curse or lose his temper. He did not sweat, even, and his skin was pure and his eyes did not tell you anything. You would not see him weep or lose himself in laughter. And if there was a moment where voices might be raised or fists drawn back, you could see him walk away. He was too careful, Tom Sebley, too careful.

Only if you watched him, hawk-eyed, owl-eared, would you have caught those moments, those some few moments when Tom Sebley lifted the blanket on his soul.

Like that time, that harvest-time, with old Mrs Cart-wright's apple wine. Bessie's mother's apple wine was famous valley-wide for its tongue-loosening, bowel-shattering, belly-warming potency. No one who drank more than a single glass of it could stand up and keep in the truth. It made you glow and warm and smile and shine and then it made you speak like it was your heart speaking, like there was a small man sitting on your shoulder taking all the thoughts out of your mind.

This harvest-time, they have all worked hard. No rain so the air is dry with dust. No sun but it is hot all the same. They work all night because the clouds are gathering and they are blacker than the devil's eyebrows and though the crop is meagre and dry, it is the only one they will get so they stay out till ten or maybe later and then finally when they can barely move another muscle, the crop is in and they too come in and collapse in the shelter of the shearing shed.

Shiny, like all the young ones, has worked hard. He does not drink the apple wine because he is still afraid of it but he sits, along with the rest of them, on the dirt with his back to the wall and he feels the bones in him, the limbs in him, the tendons, sinews, ligaments of every part of his diminutive body and wonders, God knows, if he will ever walk again.

And it is as he is travelling this odyssey of his pain that he happens to see him, Tom Sebley, only he does not look right. Something is wrong with the way he walks, the way his hands have sprung from his hips and are waving about as though he would sweep the hair from his eyes. Shiny gets up to follow him. He does not come too close. Tom leaves the shearing shed and his hands and his steps are still not right and Shiny stays behind him and he waits to see what Tom will do. And then he hears Tom Sebley speaking – to the rough fells and the dark stars he speaks and he says words that at first mean nothing to Shiny because they are soft and jumbled. He says things like shtupid and gormlessh and sheepish. He says other things like eazzy and clever and only-one and it takes Shiny all his time to decipher these words because they are strung together like shtupid-gormlessh-sheepish-eazzy-clever-only-one and they mean little. But then Shiny, with his cheerful innocent childlike disposition, he watches him and he sees that Tom Sebley is playing a game, like children do, and when he sees that, Shiny knows that Tom Sebley is talking in two voices. So he cuts the words apart and he knows that Tom Sebley is saying that they are stupid and he is clever; that they are gormless and he is clever; that they are sheepish and weakling and sappy and only he, Tom Sebley, can see the way that it must be.

It was the only time. Shiny always watched him because he and Tom were so different, because where Shiny was open and simple, Tom seemed scheming and dark and Shiny would tell you it was the only time Tom Sebley was ever drunk. He was twenty-three and his mouth ran away with him, just ran away. Most people did not pay attention or did not hear because they were too tired. But Shiny did. The fire in his eyes, the fear in his anger, the venom in his comments like they'll never be better than me – the way he spat as he spoke, the way he showed you if you were only listening just how little he thought of any of them, the way he laughed as he said over and over again they never really knew how clever he was, they never really knew. Somehow Shiny was wise enough to see that it was not just the apple

24

wine. Somehow he understood that this was Tom Sebley in the raw.

But if Tom Sebley had a soft part where the arrow could smoothe in without resistance, it was that part that housed his love for Father Standage. To Tom, the priest was a rock that would not be moved. He was grave and strong and unswerving and where in the others he saw only fools, in Father Standage, rightly or otherwise, Tom Sebley saw an equal.

And indeed, for the villagers, the vicar was an awesome figure. When Father Standage rose in the pulpit, the villagers trembled in their pews. His thick curling hair, his deep green eyes, his broad strong hands. He bellowed, he mumbled, he cajoled, he intoned. He spoke with highs and lows, whoops and whispers. He raised his eyebrows, he lifted his hands, he swung round his arms like the Messiah himself. Through every sermon, God, Jesus, all the Marthas and Marys and Jacobs and Esaus danced before the villagers' eyes. They felt the heat of the infernos, the pain of eternal damnation, the inscrutable eyes of the evil one himself.

In those days, no one dared to miss a service. They thought that they loved him. They thought Father Standage was a great preacher and a fine pastor. They thought without him they would be lost. But they did not see, for all that the empirical, undeniable truth of the Bible was made clear to them by his efforts, by his skills of oratory and presentation, they did not see that they followed him only because they were afraid, because Hell and eternal damnation and the wrath of the Father himself were prospects too frightening to entertain.

For a while, when Tom is nearing thirty, the Father maybe

thirty years his senior, the pair becomes inseparable. You see them in the valley, in the church, up in the top forest. You see the older man speaking, the younger laughing loudly, eager to please. You see a bond that is perhaps more than man to man, more than man and boy. One day, Nib Penhaligon, he sees them. Nib is the youngest Penhaligon, the gentlest. Often the hurly-burly ball of his brothers rolls over the top of him and he finds himself left behind, unnoticed. And when this happens, Nib escapes, runs out of the house and across the yard and up and away before the tyranny of his father comes crashing down across his shins, across his back, over his skull.

Today, Nib runs to the top woods. For some reason just now, his father is angrier than ever. You would think the devil snapped at his heels, you would think the devil had wormed himself inside the Old Man, started eating at his heart. Today, Nib has run and run. His breath wheezes in large circles around his ears. His cheeks sting because it is early morning and the air is fresh and Nib is hot with pain and exertion and fear. Nib struggles to catch his breath. He leans against a huge spreading oak, slowly, slowly recovering himself. In the distance, he can hear the church bells, the noises of the village but Nib comes here for the stillness, for the silence, drawn by the mists that creep in and out of the forest canopy, drawn by the smell of secret and special. Maybe today he will see a fox with her cubs, a weasel, some deer. Maybe he will catch a fresh mushroom, save a rabbit from a snare.

At last, Nib has caught his breath. He crouches down so he can hear the full extent of the forest hush. Then he walks a little, watches as the moss which carpets the forest floor bounces up from his footprints, like sea filling the sand.

He breathes deep, the mushroomy smell, the twigginess, the soft, excited quiet of the woods.

Nib crosses the stream. The current is quite strong here but there are stepping stones and he hops from one to the next. From one side of the water to the other, the woods change. On this side, there is deep. On the new side, there is brittle: there seem to be more fallen trees, only they are hidden by the moss, and in some ways it is a challenge because you can walk along and not know whether the ground is stable or whether it is going to sink down beneath your feet. A magpie rattles, for you are in her place, and then a blackbird, and you see a hare, far in the distance, drawing himself up like the soft orange-warm athlete he is.

And then Nib hears voices and it is like a pistol-shot disturbing his calm. All the magic disappears. He hides behind another oak. The voices come closer. They are unmistakeable – the creeping, snakey hiss of Tom Sebley, the chesty, hearty boom of Father Standage. Nib hovers quiet as he can. He holds his breath and in his effort to make no noise, he cannot hear what they say. The two men are close, heads together as though they are planning something. They are rapt and it is evident they would not expect to be seen. From below, he watches their backs as they pass. From below, Nib sees that Tom's shirt is hanging out.

But nothing lasts. Tom Sebley is thirty or so and his friend is thirty years his senior. Tom Sebley does not spend a moment of each day when he is not thinking about the Father. Saints days, Sundays, morning, evening prayers, Tom is there, waiting for his entrance, waiting for his proclamations, his prophecies, the power of his oratory. Between times, Tom hovers by the door to the vicarage, hoping that the Father will say why yes Tom why of course Tom and they can go for a walk and they can share some words, some laughter, some intimacy. Tom is in love. Tom is infatuated. Father Standage is the only man in the whole of the valley who is not afraid of Tom and this alone in some kind of perverse way is a compliment. Of course, in general, Tom relishes the power that he has – but in some way, he is grateful to have someone in return whom he can fear.

But nothing lasts and that October, that same October when the Old Man takes Megan on the side of the fell, Albert Hotblack goes up into the top woods to check his traps and he is just walking back down the hill when he finds the body: Father Standage, dead, clean-dead on the forest path.

For some reason, his shirt is torn. For some reason, his trousers are down but it makes no difference why he died or with whom because he is dead, clean-dead and there is, God knows, no changing that. Albert Hotblack comes down from the woods and he collects some men and they trail back up again to bring him down. For a while, they stand around him. They murmur about the state of his clothes and the site of his death. They wonder why he has died at this age, not so old after all, and in the forest of all places. They stand and scratch their heads and rub their eyes in pity and sorrow because he was a fire-and-brimstone preacher and, with his bombast and his wit, he held them together.

Tom Sebley hears that the priest has died and a curtain the colour of night comes down upon his existence. That very day, he had been with him up in the top woods. That very day, they had been together and Tom had looked up at him with wishing-well eyes and the Father had slapped him hard upon his back and Tom had felt, as he always did with the man, that he was receiving the attentions of someone who understood him.

And next thing, here they are, bringing him down from the woods and he is stiff and his face is empty. In the place of ebullience, there is softness. In the place of strength and presence, there is dead weight, indulgence, fat. Tom Sebley looks down at the priest's face as they carry him into the church and he does not believe that this is the same man. His eyes are grey. His body is huge and flat and ugly.

They hold the funeral at once. No ceremony, no fancy waiting around until his spirit has flown. Tom leads it. Not everyone has had time to come in from the fields but some kind of frenzied obsession has entered Tom Sebley and he is bent on hiding this corpse as soon as he can. He says a few words and Lysander Merritt reads a passage from the Good Book and they sing a hymn or two but the service is brief and clumsy because Tom is in charge and Tom is in pain. They take the Father outside in a coffin that barely fits the man and they lower him into a hastily dug hole and Tom throws the dirt and you can see he is all but crying, he is all but broken inside.

Others too are grieving. Mary Jessop, aging spinster, her shoulders shaking with sobs. Now she will no longer fall to her knees on the sacramental cushion and receive the bread of Christ and the wine of Christ from those fingers that every time, every Sunday used to brush her tongue, her lips, the front of her dress.

Duddon Sheepshanks and Reilly MacReilly, weeping like bairns – for who now would show them how to hook a trout, to stalk a deer, to trap a fox, show them all the things that men do, true men? The Clothiers, long-faced, sullen – they will miss the times when he dined with them because for all that he drank plenty of their wine, fairly cleaned out their larder, he was grand company and he made them laugh with his jibes about Mary Jessop and Reilly MacReilly and, most pleasing of all, about Tom.

But it is worst, the spectacle of Tom Sebley. If you had sat and watched, if you had no feeling for the priest, no sadness for the event, you would have seen his face, his eyes, his hands, his whole being. You would have seen how slack they were, how they drooped. You would have seen the sobs that racked him, every now and again, from top to bottom. You would have smelt the despair, the fear, the pain, the grief. You would almost have cried with him. You would almost have got down upon your knees and wept until all dignity, all pride poured out upon the graveyard lawn.

Gnawing, crazy grief – the kind that fills your dreams, that forms your days, the kind that makes you change from a boy to a man – that was how it was with Tom Sebley. That was what he felt when he threw those small clods of earth upon the box, heard the pebbly, empty rattle, heard the echo from within of endless death.

Inside that box was Tom Sebley's friend, the man who had breathed life into this place, the man who laughed and hunted and ate and drank and sang and roared – like a man, not a priest but a man – the man who thumped you on the back, the man whose voice filled the valley walls with its heartiness, its effervescence, its sheer unswerving power.

In the weeks that follow the Father's death, you see Tom in the village and he is empty. You see his eyes and they are set. You see his shoulders and they are drooped like leaves dying on an autumn tree. You say hello Tom but he does not even have the strength to glance in your direction.

Something in his spirit has gone. Something that he had has been taken away.

Now Tom does not sleep. He does not eat, he does not look up at the sky, he does not see where he is going, he does not utter a single word. Sometimes he sits down, sometimes he walks. He opens his heart and inside there is nothing but pain. He opens his soul and it sneers at him. He reaches out at night while he sleeps, reaches out for someone's arms to catch him that he might not topple off the cliff – but no arms come. He cries out in his dreams for someone's name, for someone to cry back but he seeks in vain – there is no echo. His man, his friend, his foil has disappeared.

And it is around this time, while Father Standage is barely rotted in his grave, while Megan is feeling with foreign fingers the contours of her growing child, while Shiny craves to return to his girl, while the sun beams through the grand rose window onto an empty pulpit and Tom Sebley's heart chills over with the pain of disappointment and loss, that he too sees Him.

Tom Sebley is wandering in the woods, walking those same footsteps that he shared with his friend that last time. He is listening to nobody, no bird, no wind, no whispering of tree leaves. He sees nothing – no golds or soft browns or dark browns, no light or dark or life. The only sound is the whining of his broken spirit. The only sights are the evanescent glimpses of something, someone who has gone. He will not ever love again – he knows that now. He will not ever be loved as he believes he was by the preacher. He will not know what it is to feel the flow of warm wine as it fills your blood, to lie back with the sun on your skin and let the clouds make tiny shadows on your eyes.

Tom Sebley slumps down. He lets the ground draw him

down in some tired resigned embrace. He lets the tree behind him press gnarled, uncomfortable bark in the small of his back. He swims in the misery that is part fear, part grief, part guilt and he sees that now of all times, he could hurl himself off the side of the top ridge and he would never care. It has been months now, months since the Father's death and still the pain has not eased. Will he ever smile again? Will he ever go back to his room in his house and feel that there is a reason to re-emerge? Will there ever be a time to look forward? The silence of the forest is disrupted by the sobbing of a broken man.

Tom Sebley – you must pity him. You must feel for his pain. He is young still but inside he feels old. Tom Sebley gets up from the base of the tree and walks out of the woods towards the rim of the top ridge. He looks down. His toes are hanging over the top. The drop is two hundred feet, maybe more. You would not live, you would not survive the fall and if you did, you would be broken in pieces by the rocks that jut out all the way down to the stony bottom of the valley floor.

Tom Sebley closes his eyes. In some ways, his pain is worse because he knows he had a hand in the Father's death. He knows that without his insistence they would not have gone there. They would not have loved, they would not have argued that last time, they would not have parted on poor terms, Tom would not have left him there with his shirt torn and his trousers down and his red face contorted in sudden spasmodic pain. All this Tom has kept secret. He has told no one and now, as he stands and contemplates his own death, it comes back to him and it will not leave his mind, this certain knowledge that Father Standage died somehow because of him. How could he possibly live with the guilt? Tom closes his eyes. He makes to jump.

Then a shadow creeps over. Maybe the sun is being taken by a cloud. Maybe there is a bird overhead or a breeze which has blown the branches down into his light and merged into something that might as well be a cloud. For a brief moment, Tom Sebley is distracted. He opens his eyes. He turns round. There is cool that is brought by the shadow, a puffing of the air, a kind of *whrrrrr* and in spite of himself, Tom looks up and he sees a horse with a man and they are riding by.

It must be nothing. It must be the pain which is making him dream unholy dreams. It must be nothing and Tom lets his eyelids down once more – it must be nothing.

But it is enough – and though his eyes close and his body braces itself, though his veins still course with the bitter waters of distress and his heart is in pieces and his will is all but gone, it is enough to bring him back from the brink of the top ridge. In spite of himself, Tom Sebley owes some tiny debt to the shadow of the coming of Nathaniel Cadwallader.

Three

In the circular pool of light that is cast by the sun as it streams through the large rose window of the church kneels a man, a small man. He is meek, cowed, sacrificial. In the cloak of his bible-black cassock, he is swallowed by shadow.

It is cold within this church and it smells of cold. Mixed in with this, the scent of must that creeps up from the vaults below, the smell of dying petals, the rich, sickly aroma of waxy wood.

It must have been a proud man who built this church. The window is exquisite in its detail, each pane both simple and glorious. The blue and yellow light, primrose and periwinkle, that pierces the glass dances lightly upon Father Duncan's crouching form. There is no sound but that of the purple cedar boughs in the graveyard as they sweep the sides of the church in the gentle winds.

Just as Tom Sebley had taken charge of the funeral, so he also took charge of the quest to find a new man to fill their church. You would not expect it but somehow, after all, he took comfort in controlling what he could no longer enjoy.

A letter was sent, then two arrived. In the tavern, Tom read out the first. Words like bishopric and diocese and lay reader. Words like remoteness and seclusion and dearth-of-candidates. It seemed they might have to wait. It seemed they might never find any man, right man or wrong man. Perversely, Tom Sebley felt the weight of disappointment.

Then Tom Sebley read out the second. It was from a Father Duncan. It said he was coming soon. It did not refer to bishopric or diocese or lay reader and it was not clear how he knew that they might need him but it seemed he could come soon. Words instead like distant and foreign and fresh. Words like challenge and improvement and together. Tom Sebley sat down. Perversely, he was disappointed once more. The wind had been stolen from his sails. He did not like the sound of the word improve.

And then when Tom Sebley saw him, when he twitched back his curtains (as they all did) on the day that Father Reginald Arthur Duncan arrived and saw this weary, loveless sprat of a man tripping uncertainly up the cobbled street, he knew, just knew that he would be no good.

The niggardly progress of the man, the hesitation of him – you would think he carried the church on his back! He is small, slight, stooped, shy. He is wispy as a feather and his eyes dart from side to side like those of a rabbit creeping down a corridor of wolves.

For a while, Tom Sebley watches from the safety of within, tweaking his curtain only now and again, only surreptitiously. But soon the temptation becomes too great and he rushes out, marches down the street to greet the new incumbent.

There is a silence in the village. No one is out, the winds are quiet, the clock hangs heavy on the day. Father

Duncan looks up from his unwieldy march and sees a hearty stomping bulldog of a man coming straight towards him. Tired, unsure, Father Duncan does not notice the twitching curtains, does not hear the gasps of stifled breathing, does not see the columns of dark eyes that are peering at him, wondering whether or not this one will be a patch on the last.

Tom Sebley holds out his hand. Father Duncan can only smile with relief. The palms of the two men meet, one girlish, pink-white hand enclosed by another that is rough and brown. In a gesture both intimate and insolent, Tom Sebley slaps the new vicar on the back, smiles with satisfaction as the stranger winces in return.

Years later, when she had time to dwell on the details of those times, Megan remembered the vicar as she had first seen him. She too had been waiting that day, sitting in the clamp of her motherhood with this child in her arms, waiting. She had not meant to stare out because she knew that was what they would all be doing. She had meant to stay in the quiet of her bothy and talk to Donald as she felt she knew she must. She had meant to swing him in the ladle of her arms and hum sweet lullabies, to swap gazes with this child, to fold her senses deep into his and rejoice in her son.

But, just as she had feared she might not, she could not love this child of hers. He did not seem to belong to her. He did not seem to call to her or even to reflect in any way the tiniest part of her. His eyes were flat; there was no brightness. It is a truth that Megan almost does not dare to acknowledge and she persists with her cradling and her gazing but the hours hang around her like lead shackles and when she glances out of the window and witnesses the encounter between Tom Sebley and the new Father, it is all she can do to keep herself inside.

And though she does remain inside, Megan inspects the new man shamelessly. Above all, she sees the pallor of his hands. Soft, so soft, they are! You never see that here. You see rough and brown, lined, calloused, stretched almost by the work. You see red and blue, you see black from the mud – but you never see white and you never see soft and, in spite of herself, Megan is transfixed.

And there is something else too, something that at first she cannot pinpoint. And she nearly dismisses it because it is so faint but her young mother's nostrils tell her there is something and she remembers now that it is fear. He smells of fear. If you looked closely – at his top lip or the lines across the centre of his eyelids – you could see beads of sweat and they were not the diamonds of a great man bracing his muscles against trees or massive sods of earth but the tiny pinpricks of a boy-man beset by fear.

Years later, she remembered how she had been struck so very forcibly by the contrast – Tom Sebley, Father Duncan. The lion and the boy. The fox and the hare.

The light dapples the floor and the man prays in fervent silence because he too sees that he has made a terrible mistake. He has come to somewhere where he could never possibly belong. He is a townsman. He is city-pink and city-shy and city-blinded.

He is afraid of these people. In the few weeks since he came, he has seen some of them – Mary Jessop and Bethan Clothier, the Joneses, the Cartwrights. He has made to smile at them, he has quivered out his hand in some gesture of embrace. He has mumbled greetings to them in the square and when they have come into the church to do the flowers or polish the pews or sweep the flagstones of all the dust and dirt that tumbles down like seed corn from the banners suspended high above, he has tried to be warm, to *make* himself feel warm, to make them see that he is good, that underneath he is a good and kindly man.

But he feels a hostility. He feels rebuked by his new parishioners. They look at him but they do not say hello and they do not seem to welcome his presence. Why, even Tom Sebley, who was in charge of finding a new priest, even he is hostile. Father Duncan knows nothing of his predecessor so he does not understand how great the contrast – all he knows is this atmosphere that is cold, churlish, ungracious.

And they do not invite him to things. Not to the tavern, not to the market, not even to the deathbed of one of their own – and surely that is his job, to welcome the souls into the kingdom of God, to bring comfort and solace to the bereaved? Father Duncan, all along a timid believer, questions his calling. He begins to wonder if indeed he is, as they taught him at the seminary, an agent of the Lord. Look out of the sacristy window and, for sure, you see the range of God's genius – the sweep of the valley, the sheer rise of the ridges, the stark sentinels of the trees, the big sky, the bright air, the birds. But where is the joy in all of this if the people within are so closed? Father Duncan longs to return to his city.

Of the few who come to visit him in those first weeks, of the few who do not just stand back, sniffing in the air to confirm their worst suspicions, there is Megan. Deathly pale, with her hair long and her cloak wrapped round her so that all

39

you can see are her eyes and her blue-tinged lips, she creeps into the sacristy with its tall-backed chairs and its shelves of books. She perches on the table. Her cloak falls open and, as it does so, Father Duncan sees the child that is sleeping on her breast.

For a moment, there is silence. The child sleeps and Megan does not speak but she is agitated, he can feel it, harrowed and jittery and Father Duncan does not know what to say or do and in his embarassment, he too remains tongue-tied. At last, the girl manages to marshal some words. She says would you baptise him Father, would you bring him into the Church? She says it urgently, hurriedly, as though if she did not say it now, she might never say it but none of this the Father can understand for how could he when he knows nothing of this place? All he sees is this girl, so pale, so troubled and he looks at her this time and he nods his head because of course he should be brought into the Church, of course he should.

So now it is Donald's baptism and, for the first time, Father Duncan is faced with almost all his congregation: Mary Jessop, coughing into her handkerchief; Bethan Clothier, Alfred Clothier with at least half a dozen junior Clothiers; Duddon Sheepshanks, Reilly MacReilly, the boys Penhaligon, immoveable foursome, subtle as oxes; Nib, huddling into himself next to the Old Man, moth-eaten hat pulled oafishly down on to his head as though that could make up for the smell on his trousers or the stubborn drip of honey that runs down the corner of his chin; the Hotblacks, Bessie's feet tap-tap-tapping because she is not good at sitting, isn't Bessie; Lysander Merritt, stick in his hand, grunting under his breath like a rattlesnake; Shiny Blackford, pale, cheerless; Tom Sebley, unreadable.

40

From where he stands in the pulpit, Father Duncan feels like a man on the cross. A thousand piercing eyes bore into him. He looks down at the words that he must say, words that he has written in haste, in ignorance and all they do is swim into one big muddle of letters. He glances over at Megan but she is engrossed in the tremble of her day and she does not see his panic. He looks up. He starts to speak. The floor is swooning up at him, the banners bowing down into his eyes, the faces melting in and out of his recognition. He says and er. He opens his mouth again but all that comes out is and er. He clears his throat in a nervous, embarrassed, exasperating fashion and says and I am sorry to be here, no delighted, of course, because it is a celebration but sorry too because my predecessor . . .

And then he tries again and he says Blessed are the meek and he tries to introduce, at this point, a stentorian tone which might carry him out of the dreadful cul-de-sac to which his nerves are leading him. He says Blessed are the meek and he goes to add to this some of the words that he learnt at the seminary but they will not come and his embarrassment grows and you can hear buttocks shifting in their pews. So he looks at the child, at this strange, slow-wit baby and he draws deep on his breath and he says Blessed be the Father and this seems to open up an avenue of inspiration for all of a sudden, Father Duncan wonders about the Father of this child and he starts to talk about paternity and about the pride that goes with it and the responsibilities of course and he looks at Megan as he does so and he sees, oh my holy aunt, he sees that he has said something dreadful, something that should never have been broached.

For even if he does not know, they do. Even if he does

not know how Megan's child, Donald, was conceived, they do – not because she told them but because how else could it have come? – and though they may not have helped the girl, though they may not have consoled her or shared at all the pain of it, they know and they do not care to be reminded about something that is, after all, to their collective shame.

Father Duncan dares to smile. He dares to look up and try to mask the idiocy of his words with a timid smile. But the eyes that he looks into are cold and uncomfortable and at once the thread of his words, such as it was, abandons him. Hastily, he spills the water across the child's head, he mutters the words, he rushes out. And then all those shifting buttocks, they rise from the pews and they walk out of the church and no one, not even Megan who is shot through with pain for the Father and pain for herself, no one says a word.

Father Duncan's nights become haunted by dreams. Never a good sleeper, now he scarcely rests at all. The iron-cold bed seems to embody, somehow, the reception that has been granted to him those first weeks. It grows spikes and it taunts him. It sits up and laughs at his predicament. How could he, an urban man, possibly have hoped to survive here? How could he, a non-believer, possibly become a man-of-God? He hangs splayed in a hall of sinners – novices, prelates, bishops troop past him in their hundreds as he languishes on his cross. They laugh at him, titter, in their hundreds. He cannot raise his hands to block his ears from the rush of hissing whispers that he knows are directed against him. He cannot shade his eyes from the smirks and the mockery. Every tortured second of his stricken faith must be endured as Father Duncan dangles in this wretched place.

For years on end, Father Duncan hangs in this hall of sinners. He is a devil marooned in a sea of satanic hypocrites. He is a sinner mocked by others stronger, more fortunate than he. He is rejected, useless, faithless, crouching in the delicate light of his new unwelcoming church, so help me God. In his nights, he yearns to escape to his days. In his days, Father Duncan prays for mercy.

To the south and west of the village is a small humpy mountain that rises from the valley floor more prominently than all the others. It is one of the many that encircle the village, soft, peachy, crisscrossed around their midriffs by dry-stone walls and thick thorn hedges. In the summer, the patterns multiply as the sheep trit-trot along the same paths, making dark grooves in the landscape. Trees rise from the hedge-lines in clutches, a few here, a few there. Now and again, your view will be broken by a small hut, stone and slate, dilapidated.

North and east of here, you can make out the more savage lines of true hills, mountains. Their colours are blacks, browns, dark purples and they cut into the skyline like knives. To the west is the sea, at times grey-black, at others red-blue. Look far, far beyond and you can see a handful of small boats fighting against the waters to wrest some bounty from its depths. No one from this valley knows these fishermen. They might be some foreign tribe, for no one but Shiny Blackford has ever left the confines of the village and its surrounding peachy hills.

In his search for some solace, in his desperate, awkward attempts to feel at home, Father Duncan walks all over these hills. Rain or shine, you will see him, bible-black cassock, head down, trudging with some dogged determination to find the joy in God's land, to see the beauty in this harsh, unpeopled place.

Contrary to his hopes, he feels no closer to the Lord here. He is afraid of this countryside, shocked by the menace of the hills, the loneliness of the sea, the meanness of the houses as they cling to the valley floor. The winds are bitter, unrelenting and when they come, Father Duncan tucks his head under his arm like a swan. Still his faith eludes him, still he hears the words that he vomits from his mouth and he feels no pride, no pride at all. Two, three months it is since he arrived but there seems no break in it, no end to the wearying solitude, the complete, uncompromising strangeness that he feels among these folk. For all that he walks every day, he does not know whether it is spring or autumn. Everything around seems soaked in the damp-grey mud that is left by months of snow.

For some reason, Father Duncan gravitates to the prominent humpy hill more than to any other. There is no doubt that the view is best from here, that the village seems both closer and tinier from this hill than from all the others. You can see the spinney where the deer live, the four jutting, granite buttresses that run the length of the church, Megan's bothy squatting in the forest of gravestones.

On top, there is an old chapel, long since abandoned, tiny, tumbledown and in front, a large wedge of lime-stone that seems to beckon you and it is here that Father Duncan finds himself planted on some afternoon. He is at the bottom of his despair, his loneliness absolute, his absence of faith never more complete. He must doze off. The wedge of limestone is smooth, encases his back and

Father Duncan rests in the shadow of the chapel wall and sleeps.

And for once, it is the sleep of angels. He is transported to a place where there is sun and laughter and azalea flowers, to a place he has not known since he was a boy wrapped in the luxuriance of his mother's long, black-brown hair. It is a place free from fear and superstition, a place where you can float and float. For the first time since he can remember, Father Duncan feels joy. His heart surges, his lungs fill, his chest expands. You would come up upon this man, prostrate upon the limestone hump and you would see the smile in his eyes, in his face, in his stretch. You can see a veil – a veil of tired, sad, low – being shaken loose.

Father Duncan feels the petals that shower him, feels the hair that enfolds him, feels the sun as it bathes his aching eyes. He feels a soft, warm breeze blowing gently over his face and as he wakes, he looks into the eyes of a horse, a tall, conker-brown stallion. The horse is breathing over him, sniffing him out. Father Duncan stays motionless. The horse is gentle, smells fine, sweet, its whiskers lightly brushing the man's cheeks as though this were a mother and her child. Father Duncan raises himself from his seat, makes to move towards the horse, to touch him. But he is gone, the image is gone, the sleep of angels has gone and Father Duncan looks out over the view.

All this time and he has waited for a sign. All this time, all that study, all those months of wanting to believe – can this be it? Can it be true? Father Duncan springs from his place of rest. He looks around and he sees that the place is after all bathed in summer. All at once, he feels the burden of his fears lift from his heart. The birds are singing, the sky is yellow, the trees are laden with blooms – it must be true!

It must be true! He has seen a sign, he has felt a sign, God is, God is! And Father Duncan knows, as surely as he has known anything, that the man on his horse has come, he has come to save them, he has come to the village and the valley to breathe the dreams of God.

Four

Soon it is not just Megan Capity and Tom Sebley and Father Duncan who have imagined encounters with this horse, this unknown man. Soon rumours begin to circulate in the village that a stranger has arrived. No one can explain where he has come from, no one can say for sure whether he is old, young, tall, short. Few of the people who claim to have caught sight of him are able to articulate their experiences. It is just that everyone feels that there is a man who has come, a man from who knows where.

Mary Jessop says she saw him in the market square one day and that he was gnarled like an old walking stick, crumpled, clothes tattered, the horse little better than some old nag. She says she wouldn't like to talk to him, no more would she, she wouldn't trust him better than she would the winds or the seas. Bessie Hotblack says she's sure he must be here why her washing came down one night, all trampled into the ground it was, with holes in it, must have been the horse as had done it. For the first time, Father Duncan steps into the huddle and a dreadful hush falls over the crowd within. Old Man Penhaligon asks him how about you, Father, have you seen this ghost of ours. And Father Duncan goes to answer but they do not let him speak because there are too many others with too many differing versions of the truth.

So at last it is Tom Sebley's turn – have you seen him, Tom asks the Old Man and Tom goes to tell them, he goes to say something or other, something to put them off the scent but all at once he finds he cannot. Those moments on the top ridge are moments he could never share. If he started to explain, he might tell them the whole story. He might say how close he came to killing himself, he might own up to the part he played in the pastor's death, he might show them that he too is only weak, is only human. Tom's tongue stays stuck to the roof of his mouth. He cannot agree about the presence of the stranger – but he finds he cannot disagree either.

And it is this more than anything that troubles them, this silence of Tom's. Everyone knows that Tom Sebley never speaks lightly, that he uses his words with care. People look up to Tom Sebley because he is the strong one, the leader. If Tom does not speak, if he does not contradict them, then it must be true. There must be a man here, a man on a horse, a holy man perhaps. And maybe he's not a man but a Goliath and maybe it is not a horse but a great Pegasus of a thing, not walking on the hills, not striding round the valleys but dancing through the clouds with the buzzards. For what else could have silenced Tom Sebley in that way? What else could have brought their loquacious leader to a halt?

And that night, their imaginations running wild, the farmers and villagers, they take to their beds with images of a man on a horse that flies with the birds, a man as large as a mountain astride a horse with wings the breadth of a river.

Part Two

One

To the rhythms of the seasons, the valley rises and falls as it always has – but put your ear to the ground and you will hear that the grasses, the trees, the birds, the rivers are gurgling, susurrating, bristling, chattering with excitement. Today is the day, today is the day.

Though everyone chooses to believe differing versions of the appearance of the strange man and his horse, though everyone in the village attributes to him widely varying powers, everyone is united behind the suggestion that they try to lure the stranger into their midst by means of a gift. Debate has raged within the tavern, night upon night, as to what form the gift should take. But it is finally and unanimously resolved that it should be that of somewhere to live – and Father Duncan, who has timorously joined the debate, he says why not the old chapel and, perhaps surprisingly, they all turn and they all agree. Why not?

Today is the day when the restoration will be complete. Today is the day when the villagers will be able to stand back from their labours and admire the fruits of their resolution. Who knows but perhaps he will come tonight? Perhaps he will see the place, hear the messages that they have planted on the winds, understand from the tunes moaned out on their Celtic pipes that he is to come here, to come and live among them? In every heart, there is a flutter of excitement. Soon they will know, soon they will see properly and they will know.

The winding hedges that line the roads that lead to the hill where the chapel sits proudly restored are festooned with garlands, ribbons, with flowers picked in armfuls and scattered here and there. Bessie Hotblack busies herself with the trees, with garlanding and polishing and shining the trees. She takes ribbons of silk hundreds of feet long that she has woven from the threads of her unravelled wedding gown and she trails them ornamentally up, down, over. As she does so, she wonders how he will be, how it will look, this horse of his, this man they have spent so long discussing. Someone said he was a huge man, bigger than you could imagine and Bessie pictures the clouds having to part and the trees to lean back as this fabulous creature, hands the size of continents, makes his way up their lane to live in the chapel on top of their hill.

Nib Penhaligon, he's in charge of tables and chairs – for the lane is to be lined with food so that when the stranger arrives upon his horse, they can sit down and celebrate in style – and he dreams of a man in chain mail and steel, swords and pistols clanking, riding in astride a horse that no man would dare to go near for fear of being eaten alive, kicked to small pieces, picked up and hurled several thousand leagues away.

Father Duncan is at the top of the hill, ensuring that the chapel and sheds are finished to his satisfaction – they are not as large as he would have liked, not for a man who might be the sign of God, but they are intricately thought out, down to the direction in which the stable door faces, down to the creation of a small granite platform around the wedge of limestone.

If he feels any guilt at the shamelessness with which he has elbowed his way to the forefront of these preparations, Father Duncan shows no sign of it. He whistles as he works. Just a few tasks to do and the chapel will be complete. Idly, as he taps in this last nail, that last rivet, he wonders how long they will have to wait. He wonders how his face will be and his hands, whether or not he will carry a sign upon his body – a prophet's thumbprint perhaps, an auspicious birthmark – that will confirm that the stranger is, as he believes, an agent of God. He wonders what he will do, *He*, and what miracles he will perform and how soon the words of the Bible will become the truth before their very eyes. Now Father Duncan, he feels he belongs. Now he looks down into the village and he feels that here is where he is meant to be. He has found a role. He has found a place where his energies, his faith, which he always knew was there, can finally be put to good use. He is a coward shown the way ahead. He is a boy at last allowed to become a man.

At one point, the Father stops – stops whistling, stops tapping, stops looking about him – for this truth, this realisation is all of a sudden home in his mind and he laughs out *HAAA*! in a long howl of relief and triumph that echoes down the hill and through the close-built houses of the village. When the stranger arrives, his idyll will be complete. Father Duncan will understand his faith. He will have seen that he was not wrong, after all, to take the path he chose all those years ago.

No one notices that Tom Sebley has absented himself from

the general excitement and flutter that is abroad between the hedge-lined lane. No one steps inside the church, not even to polish the pews or replenish the store of firewood for the sacristy. So the hundreds of flickering candles that have been placed along every beam and every lintel, upon the back of every pew and the ledge of every window go unseen. No one from the village is witness to the ritual which the tremulous Tom Sebley undertakes as he bathes in this glow, as he prays on his knees in light that is amber and golden and scarcely of this earth.

Since that day on the top ridge when he danced with his own soul, when he was brought back from the brink by the shadow of a man and his horse, Tom Sebley has been in turmoil. Why was it that he was prevented from taking his own life? Why was he saved when he would so rather have been lost? For sure, he helped them to find a replacement for Father Standage, saw to it that the village church did not remain empty – but Tom did this mechanically, only going through the motions, numb with loss and appalled at his own disgrace.

And now they want him to herald the man who prevented Tom from dying when that was all he wanted most to do, die. They want him to sing out because here is a hero, a stranger, an all-conquering, all-gleaming hero who will bring excitement, challenge, dreams to a place that has always been remote and small. They want Tom to be filled with joy. They want him to share in their anticipation. They want him to hear, as they are beginning to hear, the words that are being whispered, that this is a man from God, that he is a sign from God.

He is not bad, Tom Sebley. He is not a bad man. For years, even since he was young, he has made this village, this valley as good as they could be. He is good at organising, good at making people do their best. He says why don't we build a house and they look at Tom Sebley and they know that they can. He says why don't we all go to church and they listen and they know that Tom Sebley is right. When God shuffled his cards, Tom fell out of the pack first – a leader.

But Tom Sebley is beset by his fears. He steps outside of the boundaries which he has known since he was a child – the boundaries set by the peachy hills and the forest and the knife-sharp ridges – and he feels small. The ground stretches out before him, his height shrinks, his legs take him no distance at all. He is cowed by the rise of mountains which he does not know. There are trees, walls, sheep barely different from those in his own valley but Tom cannot help himself, he is afraid. When Father Standage used to stand at the top of the pulpit and he pointed down into the congregation – you would think eternal damnation was all you could hope for – then too Tom was afraid because he believed everything Father Standage said, he believed in the hellfire and the screaming monkeys, the flames, the heat, the endless, endless guilt and pain. And more than that, he knew as he still knows that he will not be strong enough or brave enough to withstand these terrors. In his nights, he is afraid, Tom, afraid of the dark and the noises, afraid of the bats in his attic, afraid most of all of his fears.

And now, for once in his life, Tom Sebley feels usurped. His leadership of the villagers is forced to stand back, make way because here comes something they have never had before, here comes something mysterious, unheard of. Tom Sebley does not know which way to turn. That pink weasel Father Duncan seems to have taken over his reins.

Not only has he come to fill the slot of Father Standage but now he presumes to know – better than Tom! – about the valley and what the villagers need and what there is that is about to descend among them. Tom Sebley is shocked. He is confused and hurt and shocked and he does not know where to go next, how to be next. So, for the moment, Tom Sebley stands back, he lets them do what they must do, hides in the darkness of the church and lights the candles, all the candles, and he muses.

Megan Capity, she too remains absent. These past few months have been hard for her also, so hard. All this time and she has had to dwell on the indignity, on the fright, on the pain that he caused and the pain that lingers and the helplessness. And there are consequences, of course there are, sometimes she can scarcely move because of them but most of all, there is this child, this child who seems so remote, so heavy somehow. Sometimes she wakes in the night and she relives it all, how she couldn't move and she couldn't cry out and how she seemed to have to let it happen even though it was the last thing in the world she wanted. She might wake in the morning and her teeth are on edge because throughout her nightmares she has been grinding them, rubbing them hard together in terror and shame. All her gusto, all her confidence have gone and in their place, there is little more than panic.

So maybe this man, whoever he is, maybe he will help her find a way out of the labyrinth of her fear. Maybe, if he really is a man from God as they say he must be, maybe he will be able to ease the burden of her memory. Maybe he will come as he did in her dream and he will save her once more, save her from all those images, all that relived pain, save her from all the bitterness that threatens to well up and swamp the rest of her life.

Throughout the night and the nights before, Megan has tossed and turned. She has lived and relived her dreams of him, rehearsed over and over his arrival. For the sake of the villagers, she prays he will come. For her own sake too, she prays he will come, he will ride on his majestic beast and he will see her son and he will pick him up high, sweep him into the embrace of his long, black cloak and she will know, at last she will know that his name is Nathaniel Cadwallader, that he has come among them to breathe the dreams of God.

And then there is Shiny, who should be helping out. He said he would, said he'd help Nib with the tables and chairs but he does not, only he sits down instead behind a tree and thinks of all the things that are not right any more.

Shiny remembers the day when he first met Megan, Megan when she is six, Shiny still five. Shiny is frail, short, sunlight-see-through, Megan is tall and for a girl, strong and forthright. You would not think that these two would be friends but Shiny's eyes are black and piercing and there is no doubt, if you could only see him, that Shiny has life inside of him, spirit. Megan puts her hand out to catch his because they are in the village square and some of the other boys are laughing at Shiny and Megan says here, come with me Shiny, here, let's get away and there is a weighty pause while Shiny scratches around among his thoughts to see whether or not he might dare touch this Olympian beauty. And she does not seem insulted by the delay so, in the end, he succumbs to her authority because, after all, what else was there to do?

She had a way of walking, like a dancer, with all her weight back on her heels. She had a way of shrouding him, like a warm curtain. She had a silent will which you could see would brook no opposition and Shiny used to follow her like one lamb behind another, like one wave behind another. And so they were and you would see them – in the woods, in the village square, down at the spinney – and you could barely slide a piece of paper between them because they were chatting, heads together, or they were laughing or they were imagining themselves to be man and wife, father and mother, brother and sister. They were made of the place. They breathed its fresh, green air, they blew with its driving rain-wet winds, they laughed in time to the thunder-claps which every now and then tore their sky in two.

But, more than that, you heard them talking. And it was always Shiny talking. Talk, talk, talk as though his life depended on it – as though there was never a moment to be wasted, as though they would not have the rest of their days to share their precious conversation. When he could, he said, he would go away. When he could, when he was old enough, he would get a job in another place. He would earn his fortune, make himself a rich man, make enough so that when he came back and he asked her, she would go with him and be his wife. Sometimes, his idea was to be a sailor. He would cross the seas and catch a pirate's haul, he would become a pearl fisherman, he would discover a sun-kissed island with a palace where they could live ever after. At other times, his idea was to start a mill, to build a factory, to make men do things for him, make things for him, to make them work hard as he would work hard to ensure that he had a home for his wife and their family.

Shiny has no care for the party that is being arranged by Father Duncan. He has no care for ribbons on trees or tables decked with food or celebration. Shiny longs for the girl he knew before all this happened. He longs for her smile to return and her warmth, he longs for her to let down her guard. He regrets it all bitterly, that day on the fell – what happened? What dreadful thing can have happened? He has no views on the stranger, none at all, but it seems to him as he dwells on what has been lost that it might be an opportunity – maybe they will be right after all. Maybe this man will be from God and maybe he will be able to bring his Megan back to Shiny, bring her back where she belongs.

Forks, knives, plates, goblets line the tables that line the hedges that line the lane that leads to the hill. Everyone wears his finest shirt, her smartest dress. Houses gleam, trees bow down beneath the weight of their festoons. People are standing in rows, waving banners and flags. Women beam from the triumph of their cooking, the children laugh because they have never before had a party, not like this, not with so many tables and so much food and so many banners and so much noise.

Father Duncan has begged the villagers to do this. He has gone down upon his knees in the tavern and said he is from God, I believe he is from God. He has pleaded with them do not let me down, do not let yourselves down. He has exhorted them – this is your chance, he says, this is your chance to do, to triumph and do, to welcome dreams, excitement, challenge into a place that is otherwise remote, unknown. He has wept. He has let his tears fall upon the tavern floor, beseeching them. He has found his voice, his pastoral voice and he says I know

I am not Standage but I am your servant now and I beg you, he says, I beg you. And his sincerity is there, you can hear it in his words, you can see it in his tears and slowly you are moved – Clothiers, Hotblacks, Joneses, Cartwrights, Lysander Merritt – you are moved, because it has been such a long bloody winter, because you are tired of being remote, because all you long for is another man to worship.

The afternoon wears on and there is no sign of the stranger. The smiles, the excitement become hesitant, questioning. Hopes begin to dim. Father Duncan, increasingly twittery, says why don't we start, why don't we pour the wine and eat the food, perhaps he is late, perhaps he has not heard the messages we planted on the winds. It seems an inspired idea and at once they all sit down. Lysander Merritt puts his stick upon the table, piles high his plate, flops down with a harrumph beneath the shadiest horse chestnut tree. Old Man Penhaligon does likewise, soon becomes intoxicated, remembers suddenly, briefly his time with Megan on the fell, feels a shaft of pleasure tremble through his trousers. Duddon and Reilly and the boys Penhaligon fall into the beer as soon as the Father's words are spoken and they sit together in a huddle, becoming animated, riotous, lethargic, grumpy in quick succession.

By six o'clock, the pies and tarts, the meats and fish are reduced to crumbs and bones on scattered plates. The gilt has faded from the occasion. Hair that was piled high in expectation is now dishevelled. Braces have slipped, highly polished shoes are scuffed with dust, dresses look crumpled, speech is frequently stuttering and slurred.

Megan Capity, sitting at the top of the table cradling her stiff-backed, lifeless Donald, has gradually become suffused

60

with a nervous pallor. Shiny Blackford, his eyes only for Megan, aloof, unhappy. Father Duncan, a few seats down and unaccompanied, flicking the food he languorously slopped on his plate. Tom Sebley, who has joined them at last, alone, unspeaking.

Some of the women, Bessie and Bethan in particular, have pursed their lips in triumph – they knew it was all a lot of hocus-pocus, they could have told them not to bother with all that building. They are the first to say we told you so, we told you so and they stand up from their benches, one gargantuan, the other pinched and make to set off back down the lane to their respective houses. Mary Jessop follows next, wiping her lips on her napkin. The Joneses rein their children in from the fields around, tug them by their collars and they too trudge back down the hill, muttering.

But they are all too deaf to hear how the winds are purring more sweetly. They are all too stubborn to sense the breeze that lifts the tablecloths, that ruffles the skirts of the hedges and grasses. Suddenly, the birds are flying on their backs. Suddenly, there are clouds of butterflies that hover on either side of the lane. In the distance, were you only to tune your ears, you would make out the faintest of clip-clops.

So while the feast is spent and the crowd is sullenly disbanding down the lane, Megan Capity cocks her head, lifts her eyes, says I can hear him, I can hear him and she rushes to the top of the hill and, sure enough, there he is, approaching from the far, far distance. Gradually, as he approaches, the nonbelievers lift their heads and drop their muttering. The wild flowers that line the hedgerows seem to tilt to one side, the sheep look up from their grazing, the cows stop in their tracks – you could freeze the scene in

61

your memory and it would be the same for an hour, a day, a year. Tom Sebley has dropped his glass. Lysander Merritt, for the first time in years, is standing without the use of his stick. Nib, his brothers, Duddon and Reilly rub their eyes, scratch their ears almost in unison. Father Duncan, risen from his solitary bench, drops to his knees, says thank you Lord, thank you.

Once again, Megan Capity hears the mountains and the trees, the birds and the insects whisper his name, whisper he is come, he is come, Nathaniel Cadwallader is come among us to breathe the dreams of God.

The man astride his horse rides slowly, luxuriously up the lane. Somehow, you do not see his face. Yes, he is tall and broad and strong but somehow his face eludes you and you catch sight only of his back. All you see are the long cloak that dangles on either side of the stallion's glistering haunches, the heels of his boots, the horse's thick, endless tail swinging from side to side.

People in this valley, they know about horses. Next to their children, the mountains, the trees, the winds, horses are their closest allies. Power, pure athletic power and beauty in a horse to the farmers and villagers are unmistakeable. So if you asked any of them later, any one of them to recall that moment when the man first rode up the lane to take his place in the chapel which they had brought back to life on top of the hill to the south-west of the village, everyone to a man would talk first of the horse, of the sheen in his coat and the swing in his step, of the depth of his girth and the length of his stride.

Years later, years after he had gone, the children would talk about Dungarry. They would tell each other tales of the gleaming stallion with his conker-brown coat and his sky-tall neck, of a crest as solid as oak, of a mane springing down, falling in strips, threads of silver. They would talk of his always flicking ears, of his eye so golden that if you looked into it, you'd think to lose yourself, down and down you'd go and always he's smiling.

They made nursery rhymes about him. They sang songs to his beauty and power. They said when he walked, when Dungarry walked, the ground boomed and the trees swung from side to side and the birds bounced in their nests. And when he trotted, they said, it was as though a thousand pebbles flew across the ice, you could hear it for miles. And when he cantered and galloped, they said, the trees would bow down, the grasses part like magic and even the deer who lived in the spinney would turn round to watch.

They said if he came across an obstacle – a fallen tree, a hedge, a house – you would not know that he had been there for Dungarry would fly, wings would slide out of his conker-brown sides and he would glide over the tree or the hedge or the house and you would not hear him on either side and you and the deer, you would barely believe what you had seen.

They said too, they said that the Lord God Almighty, when he had completed this magnificent beast, smiled aloud, rubbed his hands, made the clouds part with the blast of his pleasure. They said you could hear the Good Lord laugh, so proud he was, the day he made Dungarry.

Now it is night and Nathaniel Cadwallader has taken his place in the chapel on the top of the hill that has been restored for him thanks to the efforts of Father Duncan. The winding lane is strewn with abandoned plates and goblets,

63

flowers and garlands and chairs and crumbs of food. No one, not even Bessie Hotblack, has thought to clear the mess. Everyone has returned to his lair – Father Duncan to his church, Megan Capity to her bothy, Tom Sebley to his sunless cottage. A stunned unspeaking hush has overtaken them all. Most are thrilled, dazed but thrilled to the core – it is a miracle, he is a miracle! Of all the valleys, theirs has been chosen! Many take to their knees to pray – suddenly, it seems the only thing to do – so they bow down, hands clasped to their noses, saying they know not what to they know not whom.

A few remain defiant: Bethan Clothier splutters at her husband, barks at her children, makes as much noise as she possibly can given that she is sprawling in her armchair, bone idle; Lysander Merritt takes out the bottle of firewater which he normally saves for special occasions and he empties it to the last drop, rasping with indignation; once again, Tom Sebley is totally at a loss and he sits all night at the end of his bed, unable to catch a moment of sleep.

Two

In years to come, the children who were there on that day would be unable to tell you how it went on from there. How was it that Nathaniel Cadwallader in his cloak with his fine stallion came to be ensconced on that hill to the south-west of the village, came to be a part of the valley? How did it happen that the farmers, when they looked up from their work in the fields and saw Nathaniel, made no comment, just accepted the thing as normal? Even Megan Capity in her old age, blind and turning her chair to follow the sun, would be hard-pressed to describe the days that followed, the days between his magnificent arrival and those when he was just there, just one among them.

And yet, if you asked them to describe the times that followed, the atmosphere, they would have answered as one. They would have said for sure that it was grand, for sure that it was summer and the birds sang and the sun shone and the harvests were good and the stock gleamed in the light. Times had been hard, they would have said, times when harvests failed and cattle died, times when disease struck the flocks or the weather did not lighten and then they had nothing, for what were they without the food that they grew? Times when winter did not end until June, times

65

when snow fell out of a clear blue sky and everything that had been blooming was flattened into a brown flat prairie. But then Cadwallader came, they would say, and all that had been dark became summer.

Several important happenings took place in the souls of those who witnessed his arrival. Father Duncan found at last unswerving, joyous faith. At nights, when he could be sure that no one would come to disturb him, he would drop to his knees and pray, saying words that he felt, words that came to him, for the first time ever, from the bottom of his heart. You could put your ear to the great west door and you would hear a low steady hum as his words chanted forth, grateful, grovelling, certain. Father Duncan had found his faith, could believe at last. Every night, for hours at a time, he said prayers to thank God for his salvation.

Tom Sebley appeared to discover a certain meekness. He looked downtrodden. His shoulders were rounded and his eyes were dull. They put it down to his unshakeable grief, to the terrible sense of loss after Standage's death. Of course, they did not know the truth of Tom's guilt, Tom's rage at the new arrival, Tom's feeling of impotence before Nathaniel – and it is sure that if they had guessed at these, maybe they would have foreseen how it would be when Tom Sebley finally came to himself.

For Shiny Blackford, there is some hope because Megan is less afraid of him now. She lets him speak with her! She lets him hold the child, not often, mind, but now and again.

And she can do this, Megan, because she is just so relieved to find that her dreams were more than that. She is so relieved to know that the stranger was not only in her imagination, that he did come, that he did save her. And

66

more than that, it is good to know that there is something else beyond this valley, beyond the brutality of the Old Man and the schemes of Tom Sebley. Perhaps he will help them to get away, her and Shiny. Perhaps he will one day tell them how he came and they will escape and they will live out the plans they had always dreamt of. So Megan feels a lifting, a slight lifting of the pain of that day and the loneliness that followed.

Of course, it did not change her son. It did not bring life into his eyes, or joy. It did not mean that when she dangled her hair over his face or gentled him to and fro in the sway of her arms, he came to smile. But in Megan's heart, where there had been a hole of despair, where there had been a sense of isolation that was so great it was hard to describe, now there was a glimmer of warmth.

Among the rest, those Penhaligon boys and Duddon and Reilly no longer drank the same quantities of beer that they had been prone to consume in the past; Bessie Hotblack was forced to admit, to herself at least, that the damage to her washing had not been that bad, that it was probably a stray sheep or a goat; on church days when she was faced with the whole of the village, Mary Jessop took to burying herself in her Bible, no longer cluck-clucking at the front but sitting unobtrusively in a rearmost pew, lips and eyes and cheeks sucked in.

Overnight, the arrival of a stranger in their midst, some-one about whose past they remained completely ignorant, seemed to become natural. No one, if you asked them, could remember any period of awkwardness. No one seemed to feel it necessary to troop up the stony path that led to the chapel on top of the hill to veil, behind comments of welcome, ungenerous curiosity. His arrival was dreamt of, prayed for, presciently rumoured – but once he was there, Nathaniel Cadwallader became as much a part of the landscape as did the moans of the winds and the chimes of the Celtic pipes. He was a rainbow and a cloud and a ray of sun. He was the air that they breathed and the sky that touched their cheeks and the ground that they crunched beneath their shoes.

But they might have been able to describe, had they searched their memories carefully, the changes that gradually took place on top of the hill that overlooked their valley and their village. Most notable of all, though at first indecipherable, a pile of wood began to accumulate to the north and east of the chapel. Its progress was slow, probably took years. It started as just a few, some small few branches.

Nathaniel was seen to ride through the forests looking curiously, diligently for pieces of wood which took his fancy. On his walks, which had now become some kind of pleasure to him, Father Duncan would occasionally look up from beneath the shelter of his hat and see the man, his horse, a trail of twigs and branches making their way back down the stony paths towards home.

It took a year, maybe two and then the pile acquired some shape. Did you dare to go and inspect its contents, you would see that the woods were far from randomly chosen. Ash and yew, burr elm and sycamore and maple and beech – sticks and twists, straight runs, long runs, knots and wedges and blocks – each one with some unusual characteristic, some unique flaw or trait.

A pyramid grew. At first, though its dimensions were perfect, it made little impression on those who saw it. But at the end of two years or so, the pyramid was large enough to cast a shadow, pointed and geometric, over the long, buttressed wall of the church.

At around the same time, a chair appeared. It sat on the platform that surrounded the limestone wedge. When you looked up from your work in the fields, it seemed plain, large perhaps but nothing more. Its shadow was meagre compared to that of the pyramid, two twisted spikes separated by a simple span of wood.

But Megan, when she steals up there one day, seeking some few moments of refuge from the drag of her solitude, she sees that the chair is far from plain. Nine feet tall, maybe ten feet tall at the back with posts that twist and turn from the top to the floor. Mosaic of colour, mosaic of texture and shape and ingenuity. You rub your hands over the arms, smooth already from years of being rubbed and you feel that the grain is taking you, nursing your touch, soft and oiled and warm – a sleeping cat would feel so kind.

It may seem plain in shadow, this chair, it may seem unadorned but when you are up close, you see the back is not one piece of wood, not one plain old plank but thousands, millions of pearls of wood, pressed and woven together like tiny balls of silk. It glitters, it sparkles. Megan is reluctant to sit on this throne, to touch it even. It dazzles her with its intricacy. She is awed by the craftsmanship, perplexed and stunned by the majesty of its detail. For a second, the sun catches the chair full on and Megan, who has been standing on the edge of the granite platform shifting from one foot to the other, has to put her hand out to shield her Donald's eyes.

It is a village of shadows that slowly comes to people Nathaniel's hill. You could be kneeling in the church, praying in the evening light that filters through the tall, stained-glass windows along its side and you would be shrouded in shade. It might be two twisted poles joined by a plank, it might be a crown of pointing, interwoven spikes. And you would know, when it came, that the sun was dropping down its final chute towards the sea, dancing as it went through the carnival of works that were hewn by the hand of Nathaniel Cadwallader.

Just as the villagers who worked in the fields below became used to the sights of Nathaniel Cadwallader coming and going, so they also became accustomed to the chinking sounds that emerged every morning from his shed. No one thought to ask. No one seemed to say well what is he up to, why is he banging? Perhaps if they were honest, they would have admitted to some hint of curiosity.

But on the whole, they let him be. They did not visit him, they did not discuss his habits. With time, his noises and his shadows merged into the light and breath of the citrus-green valley. You hear a plink-plink-plink, you hear the moan of the wind, you see the dying, shadow-plagued sun and you know that the rhythms of the valley are fine, that everything is as it should be.

Only Megan, only she occasionally dares to climb the sponging slopes when she knows that Nathaniel is not there. She does not do so because she is foolhardy or rude, not because she is prying or desperate to know more about the man – but she goes because of Donald. Here the child seems to enter a different plain. Here, only here, the boy seems to be roused from the constant cloud of his days.

With each visit, Megan explores a little further. Today, she has dared to sit her son upon the throne. The boy, tiny

70

in its embrace, places his arms upon the chair's arms. His fingers slide down, his bottom barely touches the tapestry of its seat. Behind him stands Megan. She breathes deep. The view before her is one she could not have imagined.

The blacks and purples of the crisscross walls, the greys, yellows, greens, browns of the blowy marsh grass; the white, the pink, the barley yellow of the sky that leads out beyond the horizon; the slate-dark of the men's houses; the blue and grey of the shadow that is cast by the church. Megan sees the church in a new light. It is proud and tall and simple and from where she stands, with its size in her hand, she can see it is worshipped by the valley that surrounds it – no house is shamed by it, rebuked by its presence.

A smoky, dawny tinge has wafted in from the sea and the great west door, embossed with its two hundred and thirty-seven iron plaques, disappears. Now all you see are the colours of the valley, the church's shadow, the juniper greens of the grass that surrounds it and the heathland purples of the trees whose boughs gently, occasionally brush its vaulted roof.

Megan's eyes draw in from the valley beyond to the fields below. She sees Dungarry, tail flicking, in the sunrise gleam. Then his mares behind, the small herd that has grown from one mare to many, from one foal to several. She sees the deer, the houses and the people and the sheep and the goats and the cows and the pigs.

She sees the sights of God's pleasure: the fawn – new-born – that lies in the spinney; the weasels that have emerged from their winter furs, that are darting in the grass, eyes flashing, bodies quicksilver; and all around, the lambs, in twos and threes and ones, black heads and black toes and paper-curly coats and some are lying, barely alive, and some are standing on their mothers' backs and God is making them skip for joy because the kiss of the early spring sun will never again taste so sweet.

Megan listens and she hears the sounds of Nathaniel's days. Today is spring – God is busy in his garden – and across the woods, the rat-a-tat-tat of a woodpecker, the distant clarion of a cuckoo; far out to sea, the shouts of the fishermen, the wails of the seagulls, the chimes of a day filled with prospects; and above you, high somewhere in the great dead elm, the cricking of twigs being broken by a nesting crow – curse of the man whose chimney he will once again disable.

Megan smells, draws in her breath, inhales God's perfumes. Smells the scent from the thousand flowers, from the celandines and aconites, the daffodils and hyacinths, the multi-brilliant carpet that swathes God's land, that gleams within the view of Nathaniel Cadwallader. Smells the sweet, smells the green, smells the fresh, the warm, the new. Smells the glow on the breeze, the hope in the sky, the day that cries out God breathes in this land!

Now Megan is filled; her heart is filled. She had not known it was like this. She had not known it could be like this.

Little by little, they come to discover that Nathaniel is not just a carpenter but a woodcarver. Megan knows first of course because of the chair, because of its detail and its deep intricate beauty. Then one day, Nib Penhaligon finds a talisman, exquisite, carved from red cedar. It lies on his bunk, tucked away so as you would not see it. It smells sweet, it feels beckoning. Nib understands at once two things – that the talisman has been made particularly for him and that the man who made it was surely Nathaniel Cadwallader.

He is a youngest son, Nib, born into a family of boys all bigger, older, stronger, rowdier than he. No mother now, only the Old Man who despises Nib for his weakness, his feminine sensitivities, his lack of effectiveness around the farm. Into a family of lions is born a hare, into a basket of rocks falls a ruby. Since he was a boy, Nib has been beaten by his father. Since he was a boy, Nib has learnt to dread the very mention of the shearing shed, to know that his father was not just strict or quick to punish but a compulsive, sadistic brute.

Nib looks at his talisman. It is a tear and a smile, it is hope and it is a small trinket that he can hold in his hand to ward off the dirty thoughts of his father, the worst stings of the iron pipe. How did Nathaniel know? How did he come to discover the cruelty that the Old Man meted out when he felt like it, when it suited him? How could he possibly have known that Nib was a battered child, that he was nothing inside, null? Nib rolls the tiny wooden gift in the palm of his hand. No one has ever given him anything before. No one has ever given to Nib a sign that they knew what it was that he suffered – all his life, Nib has borne it alone. And now, here, in this wondrous minuscule gift, Nib's solitude is broken.

Nib holds it up to the light – if he tilts it just right, the sun shines through. If he looks at it with minute scrutiny, he can just make out some lettering, perhaps a biblical inscription, perhaps his name. But Nib does not need to look closely because he feels the warmth of it, he feels the relief of a burden shared, he sees the delicate care with which it has been created and he knows that this is his, that this has been made for him.

One night, when they are in the tavern together, Nib shows his cedar carving to Shiny – the winds are howling in the chimney and the ale is flowing and the noise is loud and Nib says here Shiny did you see this, did you ever see anything like this and Shiny goes over to him and he puts his hand on this piece of wood that hangs around Nib's neck and he feels warm, suddenly warm, suddenly silent, the room silent, the place hushed, the winds calm, the talking stopped.

Shiny stands still for a moment holding Nib's talisman – for a moment, he is sure he has travelled to another place – and he says why Nib that's beautiful and Nib says Nathaniel Cadwallader made it and he gave it me and Shiny says why Nib you're the lucky one and he says aye for sure for it's magic.

And then the room is silent. Tom Sebley snorts in his drink, snorts so as the ale spurts out over his nose and Lysander Merritt in the corner harrumphs, sort of growls and croaks and bangs his walking stick on the floor. Old Man Penhaligon who is standing next to Tom turns red in the face and he says with his teeth clenched and his fists all tight hush yourself Nib Penhaligon or I'll take you down the shed. Nib goes pale, white-pale and Shiny bites his lip until he can taste the warm ooze of blood as it drips down inside his mouth and no more is said about it, not then nor after.

Months later, Shiny is coming to pay court to Megan. His heart is in his mouth. He knows now. Not who but he knows what – what must have happened that day on the

74

fell. Maybe someone told him or he guessed but it does not matter because now Shiny understands. And he is afraid, today, afraid: maybe she will not be able to let him come close to her as he longs to do, maybe she will not be able to rid herself of the image of her filthy transgressor. Shiny whistles but it is not his normal cheerful whistle, more like a strained nervous *whooh* which he uses to fill the silence, to keep his mind from contemplating the worst. He wears his best clothes today, his trousers pressed and dapper, his shoes polished like glass. He thrusts his hands into his pockets because his hands, they too are anxious and he feels a small wooden lump in the bottom and he pulls it out and he sees he has been given a heart, a small wooden heart.

It is a knot of burr-elm and it has been carved lightly yet lovingly and it looks golden and if you hold it for long enough in your palm, as you must, you could swear it might beat. Shiny is deeply touched by the wooden heart. He is moved by its fragility and its brilliant expert construction and also by its texture and the slenderness of it and yet its strength. Shiny remembers the talisman that Nib received. He wonders if it has come from the same source, if indeed Nib was right, if Nathaniel Cadwallader could have made a thing of such beauty. That night, he goes to the tavern and when they are all there, he draws it out of his pocket and he says here, Lysander, have you ever seen the likes of this?

Once again, the tavern falls silent on account of Nathaniel's woodcarvings. Once again the voices are hushed and Alfred Clothier and Lysander Merritt and Tom Sebley, they all snort, they all croak with scepticism, say how it's all a load of nonsense, all a load of superstitious hoo-ha – but you can see, inside, it is making them think, inside it is making the thoughts turn circles in their minds.

Then at last Tom Sebley, whose spirits are still flagging, he finds one and it is shaped like a casket, a minute vital packet and inside, unlike the others, there is a message – words which mean something to Tom, words which are both simple and expressive. You could read these words as you choose, you could take the message as words of encouragement or words of condemnation and Tom makes his choice – Tom who is wrought with guilt and anger and now indignation – and he allows the temperature of his feelings to rise.

And then he places it in his pocket as every other recipient of a talisman does, only Tom keeps it there not for comfort but to remind him that he has a score to settle, one day, one day.

Sooner or later every man, every woman, every child in the valley is in possession of his or her very own talisman, every single one different in texture, in design, in inspiration. He seems to have the knack of giving just the right thing to just the right person. He seems to be able to foresee great crises, moments of grave personal doubt, moments of fear, moments when you must brace yourself and be brave because soon you will suffer great pain or great anxiety. Bessie Hotblack, she gets a tiny violin, barely larger than the nest of her palm and she sits down and ponders it, she tries to make it sing and she sees that maybe that was the plan, to make her sit, to make her stop busying about but rest, just now and again. Alfred Clothier, he gets one and it's like a cushion, a warm pillow, or that is how he sees it anyway, something to pull over his ears when the noise of all those children gets too loud and too much.

Some of them are scented. Some of them glow, some of them are warm, some are ice-cold, diamantine to the touch. And all of them speak to you, not with words exactly but they make you think about things, about whatever it is that troubles you. They are tiny mirrors and they show you the truth and when you hold them up, you see what there is to be seen, deep down. Just when you think that you are entirely on your own, that there is no one to think of you and support you, to hold your hand and step beside you as you march towards your fate, you find a minutely, exactly carved piece of wood which expresses perfectly the

ou must face, which enables you to fend emons and fears. It will fall out of your you will find it one day in your pocket – haligon, when you find it, you will know made for you; and you will know that the e it was Nathaniel Cadwallader.

s and Mother Theresa
heart of Ch

Three

Though she may have wished it otherwise, though she may have got down on her knees and prayed to the hills and skies that things could be altered, Megan Capity was forced to acknowledge from the very first that young Donald was no ordinary child.

From an early age, his eyes looked into a far distant place. They were flat somehow, and grey, and it did not seem to matter if you fed him or you did not, if you loved him or you did not. He barely cried, barely voiced himself and when he did, it came in a strange pitch, unholy, unhuman. You would offer him a finger that he might wrap his tiny hand around it but he would not respond. You would pick him up, love him close, smile deep into him but he would stay the same, always the same. Placid, gauche, haunting. And as he grew from babe to infant to small child, he did not change – always the same, always within himself.

Almost overnight, it seemed, he grew. He was big – huge, in fact – and people who did not know him, Martha of Morland when she first came to the valley, Archie Jessop's cousin, Arnold when he came to visit, they assumed at once that he was stupid. From barely two years, his back was broad, hands muscular, legs stocky. His size lent to him an air of oafishness, even to one so young. It made him appear slow and clumsy. They looked at him and all they could see was size.

All the same, Megan did her best by her son. She wrapped him in the warmest blankets, dressed him in clothes made out of the best fabric she could find. Every day, while he was still in arms, she put him in the donkey cart, hitched up the colt, rode about the valley, pointing enthusiastically look Donald, look at the blackbirds, look Donald, look at the fawn, look Donald, there's Father Duncan! Just as the coming and going of her sheep and her goats, the ringing of the church bells, the chiming of the Celtic pipes, so the crunch of the rickety wheels and the tip-tip-tap of the donkey's hooves became familiar to the villagers, part of the sing-song rhythm of their daily lives.

Then, once he could walk, she took him to the village square to play with the others. You could see he was not right because when they came towards him and asked him to join in, he barely seemed to notice their presence – he would just hide behind his mother's skirts or he would stand there with a fleshy lip hanging out and nothing you could try, no amount of cajoling, would make him do otherwise.

Some days, Megan would catch herself watching out of the window, gazing at him. He would be running in the garden, chasing the lambs or Daisy's latest batch of kids. She could say to herself he is fine. She could catch the glimmer of a smile upon the boy's infant lips and she could say it is not that bad, he is not that bad. But then, all of a sudden, he would be drawn to the edge of the well that lurked at one side of the grass and he would peer right down into the depths of it, leaning over the edge of the hole, leaning into its jaws as though he wished to be swallowed. There was no fear, no sign of fear and Megan would shudder, afraid to shout out, afraid to cause what Donald seemed almost to embrace. Then at last she could tear herself away from her fears and she would rush out to the garden screaming Donald, step away from there, step away from there!

Not long after he had learnt to walk, Donald disappeared. Megan lost him, totally lost him. Oh my Lord, this is it! Megan is frantic. A bolt of fear lances her chest. Where on God's earth has he gone? The well! She hurtles down the garden, squats over its yawning chasm. No sign. She runs up and down the stairs of her bothy, out of the garden into the churchyard, up to the path that leads to the fells, down into the village, all around calling Donald, Donald, frantic, thunderstruck, terrified.

No response, not a whisper so she takes her search further, pell-mell, no logic, just running hither and thither, all the time hollering his name, round the village, into the church, the tavern, round the valley, up the hill to the top forest, down the way towards the sea and now it is growing dark and Bessie Hotblack and Bethan Clothier have joined in the hunt for they have heard the hollering, everyone has heard it and they are haunted by the cries of a mother searching for her child.

Soon the men come too and the children and then they are all there, walking up and down and up and down the village and the valley calling for Donald Capity, calling for Megan's child son who has vanished like a puff in the wind. Right into the night, long after darkness and the bats have come and the owls are hooting, long, long into that longest of nights, the villagers and farmers of the valley search the length and breadth of it looking for Megan Capity's missing son. They search until they can search no longer, until they are so tired and their voices so hoarse that even if they wanted to, they could not walk another inch, could not call out not even once more Donald Capity, where are you, Donald, come home.

Not a squeak, not a hint of him, not a piece of torn trousers nor a fragment of a toy, not a whimper, not a hint any single where that a boy just two years old has been there, is lost there, is hiding there, has been taken by a fox or a badger and been eaten there.

Everybody falls into bed, Megan into hers, too tired to weep, thinking well that's it Megan Capity that's just it, you've gone and lost your son, clean lost him.

In the morning, Megan is up and she is dressed and she is thinking oh my God, oh my lord, Megan Capity, you've had the nerve to sleep when your boy is missing. Rushing here and there, what do I do next, where do I go when she just happens to look in on his bed and there he is, sleeping as he should have been all along, under the covers, his hair in a tangle, his eyes fast closed, not a clue that he has been crying or worried or distressed and his clothes are on the floor in a heap and his shoes and his socks and Megan sits down on the end of the bed while he is still sleeping and she weeps till her eyes are red-dry and her heart is all wrung out.

And it is on this dreadful day that Megan finds her very own talisman. She is spent from emotion, from fear and relief and guilt and she goes to take out her handkerchief, exclaims aloud why, what in the name . . . ? It is a flattish piece of wood, very dark, not ebony but rosewood, perhaps, or walnut or mahogany that has been well weathered. It is smooth, smooth as though you have held it in your hand every day for a thousand years. Flattish, on one side quite level, but on the other, there is a gentle curve like that in a shallow bed or a lily leaf and you can see, quite clearly, you can see the mark of a small child that has lain there. The child has pressed itself into the leaf and slept, sheltered and safe.

When she sees it, Megan is lost for words. Somehow, in this tiny wooden icon, she sees all the pain and all the hardship that she has endured these past few years. Someone has understood just what it is that she has suffered. Someone has known all her anxiety, they have known the humiliation and then the guilt and then the worry and now the fear that she has for her son. Someone has seen her from the inside, not as she seemed to others but as she was, as she has been. With that single understanding, Megan takes another step up towards the light. Someone has seen her as a woman. Someone has understood her trials as a girl, as a woman, as a mother. Megan sees her talisman as a gift, a thing to be cherished, a pearl and years later, when all this is over, she takes it out and holds it up to the sun that warms her blinded eyes and great fat tears of regret fall upon her lap.

No one ever found out where Donald had been all that time while they shouted out his name and searched the valley high and low. No one ever knew where he had been, not until twenty-odd years later, that is, not until after they brought him back down from the swanny-pool.

Slowly, they came to accept this habit that Donald developed when he was as young as two – of disappearing. He would go missing and you could search and shout and worry and weep all you liked but you would never find him, never. Megan said she might as well cry herself to death for all the good it would do her.

But after that first time, when everybody had come together, people in the village were different about Donald. Somehow, they came to share the guilt of him. All this time and no one had ever said a word to Megan. It had been some kind of dirty taboo subject. No one ever said to her that they were sorry, no one ever asked her who it was or promised to break the man's legs. Perhaps they were afraid, perhaps she was too proud, perhaps it was too close to owning up to something, they knew not what exactly but something. And then they had all been given a fright and it was as though that was the shove they needed, just to ease her lot a little, just to help her shoulder the burden of her uneasy child.

To Megan, this change was both unwelcome and welcome. Unwelcome because what if they decided to be kind to her too, what if they decided that she should take them into her confidence? What if they wanted, now that they had in some indirect way broached the subject, what if they wanted to know Who It Was? To Megan, the thought of uttering his name to any of them – to Bessie, to Bethan, to Shiny, above all to Shiny – was abhorrent. Then what kind of feelings might she unleash? What other confessions might she make? Might she spill out all that she went through in her mind since that day? Might she share some of herself, when she was at her lowest ebb, and then be forced to live with the knowledge that they knew her more than she would ever know them?

On the other hand, Donald as he grew up became an increasing burden on his mother. She felt constantly the weight of his thickness, of his remoteness. He was beyond her, every day grew further from her. Was he clever, stupid, tormented, happy? She never knew. Soon her fear for her son outweighed her pride and in the end she was grateful, daily more grateful for the way that the villagers – the Hotblacks and the Clothiers, Father Duncan, even Duddon and Reilly – tried to help him, the lad.

Nib, for one, he taught him fishing. Took him to the swanny-pool, showed him how to dangle a line, wait for the tickle at the end, wait till just the right moment, not too soon, not too fast. And Mary Jessop gave him tasks, clear the garden, move some logs, watch the birds for me. Father Duncan went round the churchyard with Donald, spelt out all the names of all the dead, told him some of their stories. Albert Hotblack let him help with the pigs and the cows, let him carry the hay to them and the water and Bessie, she too joined in, showed him how to bake bread, how to make stews, how to cook cake for the birds in winter.

Even Lysander Merritt, generally speaking a terror to all the children in the village, so sour, crusty as an aging reptile – even he made time for Donald, showed him how to take a piece of sheep's horn or a knot of wood and turn it with his sharp knife into a sheep's head or a game bird to top one of the hundred bits of ash that he kept stacked throughout his tiny butt'n'ben. Donald came home sometimes with a miniature walking stick that Lysander had made with him, proud he was of his stick and Megan was pleased.

And, yes, for this, for these days when he smiled, she was grateful.

But of all the villagers, perhaps it was Tom Sebley who made the most outstanding effort with Donald. Though he did not know for a fact who Donald's father was, Tom Sebley had guessed. He was always sharp, Tom Sebley, ferrety. To begin with, he had thought he might use this information, divined though it was. But for one thing, he was afraid of Old Man Penhaligon; and for another, he was a little in love with Megan Capity.

To his own surprise, Tom Sebley kept his thoughts on

Donald's conception to himself. More surprising still, he became the lad's friend. He took him on walks, showed him how to search for truffles and stone rabbits and pick fish up out of the river with his bare hands. Soon he was talking to the boy about all the people in the village, all the secrets he knew, all the secrets he had gleaned over the years. At last, he came to talk to him about Megan, about the way her cheeks gleamed, how her chest swelled, how her arms were rich and slender at the same time, how she laughed, how she looked at you, how she was proud, kept herself to herself, how she was a fine cook and a good mother and decent.

And Donald did not respond, neither chided nor praised Tom but appeared simply to listen, so Tom became freer with his admissions, confided in Donald everything, every tiny detail of his admiration for Megan, of his resentment of Father Duncan, of his disgruntlement at the way things were, of his contempt for *him*, of the plans that he had to go back to the good old days – so that soon, in the length of a few years' acquaintance with Donald, Tom Sebley had opened up entirely to this unspeaking, unloving boy.

You might think that Tom Sebley would come to despise Donald – you do not love your confessor – but it is not so. Tom comes to need the boy – where else would he find anyone prepared to listen to him for so long, so free from judgment?

They all made a special time for Donald. They grew used to his silence and his sombreness, to his bulky presence. Some loved him, some feared him, some depended on him. But, for all that, they knew, everyone knew, Megan and Father Duncan and the Hotblacks, they knew that it was not enough. They did not stop Donald from disappearing, sometimes for as long as a week at a time. They did not truly reel him in from wherever he went when his eyes clouded over and his words dried up. Somehow, for all their efforts and their willing it so, the villagers could not do enough.

As years passed by, as Donald grew and his trousers crept up his legs, it became clear that the only time when the child came out of himself, the only time when he seemed to have some glint of recognition in his eye were those days when Megan took him up the limestone hill to the home of Nathaniel Cadwallader.

She did not take him every day. She was afraid of becoming a pest, afraid also that one day she would slip up and Nathaniel would be there and she would have to endure the frantic embarrassment of meeting the man who was so much better confined to her dreams. In some way, it also worried her that she might lose Donald to this hill. He seemed different up here, so much at ease – and it was a transformation so great that, for some reason, she recoiled from it.

But then, every now again, she would look out of the window and she would see the sun high in the sky and the gulls floating on the breeze and maybe there would be a hare or two in the top fields and then she would say right, Donald Capity, off we go.

Off they would set, Megan in her best pinny, and she wraps one of her apple pies in a muslin and away they creak and scritch and clop, Megan and Donald and the black donkey, out round the bottom of the village and down to Nathaniel's hill. They reach the gate in the five-mile hedge and Megan steps out of the donkey-cart. She has to drag him up by the fingers with his feet digging a groove in the pathway, not screaming he is, just flopped and thick and numb because sometimes he is like this, just a dead weight. She begins to wonder why she is trying so hard to make him happy when all he appears to want is to be left alone and by the time she reaches the top, her cap is drenched with sweat and her arms are aching and her pinny is crumpled and dirty.

She calls Nathaniel, Mr Cadwallader but there is no answer. She says to Donald he's probably out with the horses, with Dungarry and she calls out again Nathaniel, Nathaniel Cadwallader, praying that he is not here so that she can walk with Donald to the wooden throne and sit him there or circle the five-mile hedge and suck in the view. Perhaps he is out gathering wood, she says brightly. And they trundle off to the granite platform, only now Donald does not have to be dragged and Megan is beginning to feel the calm that comes over her when one of these moods has passed, when Donald is no longer an unexploded lump.

At last, one day when Donald is about seven and they have tiptoed up the hill for perhaps the second time that year, Megan miscalculates. They leave the donkey and trap at the gate, they reach the summit of the hill, Megan calls out as she always has and this time there is a harrumph and she realises that he is there. Megan is stricken with shame and guilt. How could she possibly have the temerity to intrude on another man's ground? How could she have dared to presume that it was alright for her to take this leaden ox of a son up to another man's place to sit in his chair? Megan makes to tidy her pinny, to shake down her hair, to cover her confusion with some tiny veneer of composure. She goes to say Mr Cadwallader, I do hope you will forgive me, I do hope that we have not . . . but her thoughts do not have the chance to form themselves because Donald has disengaged himself from his mother and he has gone to the source of the sound and for a full ten, fifteen minutes, Megan stands there and she does not hear a thing. Donald, she goes to say, Donald Capity, come back here. And she goes to move from where she has been rooted to the spot, to drag him out backwards by his hair if she has to from the interruption of the poor man's work – but she does not need to because after the silent ten-, fifteen-minute pause, the boy reappears and he says to his mother it's alright Mother, I can stay. And Megan is so shaken by the fact of his addressing her, by the fact of her normally tongue-tied son articulating something approaching a sentence that she turns on her heel and walks back down the hill to where the donkey and his trap patiently await her return.

Later that day, Megan steels herself to go and retrieve him. She is trembling with nerves lest she has lost her son, lest she meet Nathaniel, lest she find after all that Donald is just the same. Who knows why but it is all she can do to keep the reins calm upon the donkey's back.

But she need not have worried because Nathaniel is not there, because Donald is waiting for her, because the sun is going down in damson reds on the glittering sea and there he is, waiting at the edge of the hill, a piece of wood in his hand, a wide, wide grin on his face. Megan has never seen Donald smile so. He was never like that, Donald, never. You've never seen him smile like that, she told Bethan later, forgetting herself. Never!

Donald smiles so wide that his teeth gleam in a broad white band and somehow they catch the evening sun and you can see this sharp red flash across the valley, so bright that Father Duncan, who is praying in the churchyard with his eyes pointed heavenward, has to shield them with his hand, so bright that all the sheep on the hillside look pink in the glow of it.

Megan walks towards her son, so lifted inside that she can barely hold herself back from laughing, and she goes forward and heaves him up and hugs him and for the first time since he was a tiny infant child, she feels that she can love her son, love him as a mother should.

That night, Megan invites Shiny to the bothy. It is the first time that she has dared to let any man come within her boundaries but she has to tell someone, she must tell someone who will understand. Megan says that Donald does not stop smiling all that night, that he is so excited by his day on Nathaniel's hill that he sits up for hours, on his mother's lap, and he talks in a babble for hours about Dungarry and the mares, about this filly and that colt, about the chapel and the chair and the woodpile. And Shiny, who is thrilled to be in the bothy, he listens while she too babbles on and he smiles because this is where he should be, this is how it should be.

And while Shiny sits downstairs and talks to Megan, while they share the excitement of it all, Donald sits in his room and rolls in the palm of his hand the perfect wooden carving that he has today been given by Nathaniel.

Somehow, Nathaniel must have known what it was to be like Donald, what it was to be closed inside of yourself, to show no feeling, to have no words. Somehow he must have sensed how alone Donald felt when the other children spoke to him, taunted him, asked him questions and Donald could not respond because he did not have words or any sense of how to be. For the carving, Donald's own talisman, is the gift of speech. It is the gift of words, the gift of feeling, the joy of sharing something that you have with someone whom you love. It is a tear and a smile – a tiny polished ingot that says you are cared for, you are not alone.

In a way, Donald responds to his talisman as Nib does. He is proud of this because it is the first time he has ever received a gift. But also he is proud because a man like Nathaniel whom everybody holds up as a hero has noticed Donald, a boy. Donald clasps this treasure in his fingers. He does not know about God or the complexities of adults' needs. All he knows is that someone has sensed exactly how it is to be a boy like him and Donald swears, upstairs in the bothy on his bed, he swears he will never let this tiny wooden gift out of his grasp.

And years later, when they brought his body down the hill from the top forest, they found Donald had been true to his oath for the only thing left about his person was the talisman, hanging from a small string around his neck.

The following day and for many days after that, Donald tugs Megan's sleeve and begs with his eyes, jumps up and down beside her until she has finished her chores, baked her pies, fed her goats and sheep, polished her floor, until she can take him back up the hill to spend another day with Nathaniel Cadwallader. It is so good to see Donald like this, to see his eyes clear and some of the pain that seems to be within him gone.

And every evening, when she has fetched him down again, when they are seated back in the comfort of the bothy, Megan asks him what have you done today my Donald and Donald, who has been longing for his mother to ask this question, barely draws breath for an hour, two hours, three. He has carved the wood and held the chisels, gone on walks up in the top forest or down on the beach, hitched up the clunking chariot, held the reins, chosen this bit of wood or that bit, brushed Dungarry, brushed his face and his nose and his great crested neck, led out the mares, fed the foals from his hand.

Before long – though every day Megan climbs the path and leaves an apple pie wrapped in muslin upon the pearl-embedded chair – Donald does not come down the hill but he lives there for days on end. Only now and again, he ventures down the hillside to see his mother, to show her what he has made or to tell her what he has done. And when he does, the villagers and farmers, they cannot believe that this is the same child, the same lumpen boy whom they used to take turns to amuse. There is a spring in his step. He has grown and yet he does not seem big now, just tall. There is purpose about him, his eyes are clear, no longer clouded and remote. Albert Hotblack, Mary Jessop, Tom Sebley above all rejoice to see Donald Capity so. Perhaps it was not so bad after all, they say in their secret hearts, perhaps he is not so bad.

In these times, Megan dusts the top of her apple pies, once they are baked and golden from the oven, with the essence of her everlasting thanks. It is as though someone has come and lifted a great boulder from her heart, lifted it and thrown it to one side. Now, she can tend her sheep and work the garden and grow the vegetables and at nights she is able to go to the tavern, just once or twice, and she lets Shiny hold her hand and together they sit and the warm ale burns their gullets and her eyes sparkle. At night, she prays in thanksgiving, prays for Nathaniel Cadwallader who breathes the dreams of God.

Four

In these golden times, Nib Penhaligon too is granted some kind of salvation. The Old Man is struck by a paralysing stroke. One moment, he is trimming the feet of his ewes – quite gentle he is with his ewes, the Old Man, you would be surprised, he lifts them over his knee and cuts the foot so quickly that before you know it, the ewe is back on her feet, not so lame now because the Old Man has been clever and cut out the rot, eased the pressure, given her a new lease of life – and the next, there is a great cloud of numbing smoke that fills his brain and fells him there and then upon the shearing-shed floor.

Anyone who knew him and who knew medicine might have guessed that Old Man Penhaligon was about to have a massive stroke. Over the past few nights in the tavern, he had been talking, more than usual, not taciturn nor growling like always but garrulous and garbled. In its way, this uncharacteristic, voluble Old Man was entertaining because the words came out all tripped up, illogical and confused.

Every night for one ominous week, Old Man Penhaligon came into the tavern and burbled. Mostly, it made no sense, became more idiotic and hard to follow as the week progressed but Duddon and Reilly and Lysander and Tom especially enjoyed this spectacle, enjoyed the crazed images and the wild associations which seemed to pour unending from the Old Man's mouth.

Towards the sixth day, the tone altered, became bawdy, lewd, disgusting. Still, the tavern regulars laughed at him, egged him on. They might have known that Old Man Penhaligon was not right. They might have seen in his eyes that though he was speaking a great deal, holding forth, the man behind those eyes looked perplexed, alarmed. They might have sensed, had they cared to, that he was speaking so volubly not because he wished to entertain but because he was trying and trying and trying again to say the one simple thing that he wanted to say.

If they had only stopped to consider, Duddon and Reilly and the others, they might have felt sorry for the Old Man, they might have tried to help him now, here in the tavern before it was too late.

But just as he took his bendy iron pipe again and again and again to his youngest son, just as his lip curled with pleasure as he walked away from the rape of Megan Capity, so the Old Man had beaten or worsted each of them at one time or another. He might have been a young boy, ten years old, and cornered one of them behind the school, ambushed him with a whip or a stinging baton. He might have been an adolescent, small but wiry, challenging one of them to a fight in the shed, hiding up his sleeve some object which made his fists harder and his blows doubly difficult to withstand. Or maybe it was when he was a man, a farmer and one or other of them strayed into his land, unwittingly crossed him by doing this wrong, that wrong, looking at him in a way he did not like, saying something he would not agree with. Depending on his mood, he might just have dreamt up a reason but in some way or another, he had found the opportunity and the authority to vent his bitter phlegm on virtually every one of their fated hides.

There was no conspiracy, no conscious will to round on him, wreak old revenge – but tangibly, silently, these men who sit around him in the tavern every night for one word-garbling week ignore the signs that Old Man Penhaligon is heading for a fall and they enjoy instead the details of his descent.

When he finds his father sprawled upon the shearing-shed floor, Nib is overwhelmed with remorse. How long has he been lying here? Two days! Nib knew the evening before when the Old Man did not come back as usual that there must have been something wrong. He knew but for some reason, he just sat there and said to himself well he's probably too tired or he's busy still on the fell or he's staying over in the shed because he just cannot face the long walk home. He knew that this had never happened before, that the Old Man always came home but just for once it was a relief not to have to sit there, not to have to sit on his bed and listen to the way the door was banged shut and know whether or not he was in for another hiding.

So now Nib finds the Old Man lying face down on the shearing-shed floor. He turns him over. The body is limp and Nib for a moment fears the worst but then he hears the short rasps of his breath and he sees a faint movement in his eye. Does he speak? Nib shakes his father, he shouts out – why should he care after all the Old Man has done to him? – but Nib is frightened, filled with guilt and, God alone knows why, with pity.

See how the tables of fate can turn. Here is the Old Man, the same one who singled Nib out above all of his brothers for the worst, the most violent and unbridled beatings, now lying lifeless in the arms of his youngest son. Carefully, gently, tenderly, Nib lifts his father between his arms and carries him back to the farmhouse. He lays him on the kitchen table, reaches for a cloth and wipes his mouth, goes upstairs, digs out some blankets, rushes here and there seeking things that might help to ease the Old Man's final predicament.

In the days that follow, a banging-tapping-clanking issues from one of the Penhaligon farm sheds. At last, Nib emerges. He has constructed for his father a chair that can be wheeled about the farm. It is monstrous, lopsided, rustical, rough to the touch, wide at the front, narrow at the back, attached by some curious, clumsy mechanism to the abandoned chassis of an old hay-cart. The edges are unfinished, the height is arbitrary and asymmetrical.

All the brothers, when they come in from the fields and the tavern and their days outside, take one look at their father in this preposterous contraption and they laugh at him, mercilessly, pointing at the way he flops to one side, at the way he cannot control his head, at the way a puddle builds up on the floor beneath because he has lost control of everything, every single part of his body. He is no longer a man now, Old Man Penhaligon. The brothers mock their father. Pah, they jeer, look at you!

In the quiet of the day when his father is sitting out in the sun and the brothers are working in the fields, Nib nestles in the cool of his room. He sits on the furthest corner of his bed, his arms wrapped round his knees, rocking back and forth, back and forth. In the palm of his hand, he clasps his talisman. He does not know whether to be thankful or not, joyous or not – for the very roots of him have been severed. Only with the carving in his hand does he feel reassured. With the carving in his hand, he can always remember and the guilt from his joy can be assuaged.

And outside, beneath Nib's window, the Old Man sits in his chair. The weeds that grow between the cobbles in the farmyard blow in the breeze, brushing the ankles of Old Man Penhaligon, brushing back and forth, back and forth until they cause pale pink abrasions on his papery skin.

Few of the villagers come to visit Old Man Penhaligon now that he is confined to a chair. Too long has the Old Man's tyranny bitten into their pride. Lysander Merritt comes once, more to peer at the victim than to sympathise with him. Tom Sebley comes, of course – he is a little horrified by the sight of the Old Man, shrinks back from this rotting carcass with its smells and its unwanted excretions. But he is pleased to see him like this because Tom too was afraid of the Old Man, afraid of his vile temper and his volatile fists.

Father Duncan also calls. He brings a prayer and a fitting word, douses the Old Man's head with holy water, pats Nib on the shoulder, leaves rather hastily because he is embarrassed somehow, only he cannot remember why. Next Megan – she does not spend much time in front of the Old Man but she does bring with her an apple pie and for this, so simple a gesture, Nib grants her a timid smile. But Duddon and Reilly and the other young lads, the ones he used to drink with and cuss with, they do not go near at all. Sometimes they sit in the tavern of an evening and wonder what has happened to Nib but mostly they carry on as they did before, no consideration for the very tiny tragedy that has taken place in their midst.

Then, one day, Nib hears footsteps in the cobbled yard. He gets up off his bed, wanders over to the window, peers out to see who it might be. Nib is too slow and before he can do anything about it, the boy Donald is standing at his door. Why has he come? Nib cannot hide his surprise. It is an awkward moment.

Donald does not speak and Nib flounders in his ungainly presence. Then Donald leaves the room and goes downstairs. Nib watches him from the window. He sees Donald walk over to the chair, clumping like he always did, clump, clump. He sees him trip over one of the cobbles – there is a scattering of dandelion seeds – and almost laughs.

Donald walks round to the front of the chair so that the Old Man can see him. Then he stands there, silent, not even a flicker of his eyebrows to suggest that there is any line of communication between the two. Nib does not understand this scene that is played out before him but he is perplexed by its duration.

For what must be an age, Donald does not seem to move nor even to make a gesture. Silent and motionless like the Old Man, he stares and stares and stares, dull eyes into dull eyes. Then at last he reaches out to touch the Old Man – and Nib is astonished for he sees, he is sure that he sees that his father, with what must be one gargantuan effort of will, recoils so violently that the wheels of his hideous, cumbersome chair are jolted over one cobble, back on to the one behind.

Now and again, when Megan and Shiny have a spare

moment, when Daisy and the sheep have been grazed and the chores are done and Megan has climbed the hill to deposit her apple pie, they call on Nib and offer to take his father for a brief turn around the farm. And because this is the golden age and the spell of Nathaniel Cadwallader is at the height of its powers, Megan is not triumphant nor gleeful nor relieved when she sees Old Man Penhaligon so, being wheeled about the valley in his grotesque lopsided cart with his head lolling and his eyes sightless. She does not even relive, though well she might, the pain that those few minutes have caused her in all the years since, the loneliness, the empty stomach-clawing guilt.

She does not dare to ask herself why she comes, how she can possibly bear to share the same air as her transgressor – but she comes all the same, and Shiny comes too and together they push him around the churchyard, stopping at each of the headstones, resting under the heathland purples of the swinging boughs above. Or they drive him down the lane to the Hotblacks, chat to Bessie and Albert over the hedge. The Old Man does not respond in any way to these outings. Sometimes, you might think that there was a tear running down his cheek. Sometimes, you might think that his leg muscles were taut, as though he were bracing himself against something. But mostly you do not notice. And in any case, you are busy and you do not need to open that cupboard because it is only murky inside, only murky.

One day, Shiny and Megan plan a picnic. They mean to go to the gate that breaks in through the five-mile hedge, to eat on the grass, then visit the horses, say hello to young Donald, deliver a basket of food to Nathaniel. It is a beautiful day and for some reason, Shiny says to Megan we can take him with us.

The sun is beaming down, lying on his back with his hands behind his head, stretching for the joy and the thrill of it. The grass is green in our valley, green and filled with hope. These are the days, these are the days! Shiny brings around the old donkey cart and he hoists the Old Man out of his lopsided chair and on to the bench at the back. Then he must secure the Old Man to ensure that they do not lose him on the bumpy track that leads up to Nathaniel Cadwallader's so Shiny finds some old scarves that he had once given to Megan in the days when he was going to be a big trader and she was going to go with him to other places. The scarves are silk – yellow and gold and some red and some green and some many-coloured. There are long ones and short ones, thin and broad ones. Shiny laces them round the Old Man, tying him to the arms, propping up his head with a fragment of ewe-fleece.

This is the day, this is the day! Shiny and Megan sit up front. The black donkey reluctantly tip-taps forward and the cart creaks into action. Megan has a basket filled with picnic. On this of all days, there is a spell in the air. On this of all days, Megan is charmed, Shiny is charmed, the valley is charmed. There can never be a better time. The sky is azure and the smells are of orange blossom and lily-of-the-valley and of honey and mist and rain on a warm earth. The lime trees are iridescent, the horse chestnuts are bowing down with flowers, all around is the buzz of an awakening earth.

Shiny flicks the reins down the donkey's back. He looks across to smile at Megan, she returns his smile, smile of an old friend, old, old friend. The track is bumpy, donkey moves slowly, tip-tip-tap, cart boings and clunks across the stony ground. Shiny and Megan chatter, catching up. He tells her about the farm where he works, should they keep the white bull, should they use the black one, should they eat the vicious rooster, will the sow farrow this day or that.

Then they are there, they have reached the five-mile hedge, they shout to the top Donald, Donald, unfold their picnic upon the grass, eat, chatter some more, wander off looking for the boy, the man, the stallion and his mares. Climb the hill, no one about, marvel at the beauty of the throne, sit down, lie back in the sun, drift through the afternoon, revel in God's beauty.

She says to Nib after, when they have come back down the hill, returned the Old Man home to the safety of his chair and his weedy cobbled yard, she says they had a grand day, grand day.

But when she and Shiny are back within the safety of her bothy, she confesses her shame, her guilt. Throughout the day, that whole searing hot day, they had not given him one thought! Without so much as a backward glance, they had left him there with the yellow and scarlet and blue and green scarves blowing in the breeze, strapped flat to the cart, donkey scratching about impatient, left him there, not fed him, not eased him, not even looked round until they got back down from the hill and saw him red as a beetroot, gasping, a swarm of mosquitoes buzzing in his helpless eyes. She says, I never dared to hate him, you know. She says it without thinking.

And Shiny looks at her and all at once, he knows – not just what but who.

Five

When Megan Capity is old, alone in the village and the valley, with only the turning sun and the echoes of the endless winds to keep her company, she reflects ceaselessly on these days.

Those times, she could see, were the golden age of the valley, the very height of its golden age. From a time of dark, a time of ignorance and roughness, her village came into the light. It had discovered itself, discovered the good and the bad, opened its eyes. In these days, the sun never set and the grass only bloomed. A spell was cast – by the magic of Dungarry, by the magic of Nathaniel's woodcarvings, by the transformation of Donald Capity. The villagers and farmers believed in this magic, embraced it, every day awoke and saw new beauty in their land, new promise in the way that the winds blew and the blossom flowered and the birds floated on the warm air.

In these golden times, the bumpy track that led to the five-mile hedge that surrounded the hill where Nathaniel Cadwallader lived with his tools, with his horse, with his work, was ridden over many times by many feet and many wheels, carts and carriages and small shoes and big shoes and boots and hooves. People came and went, gently, on

Sunday afternoons or on special days when it seemed good to celebrate. They did not always climb the mountain. They sat in groups among the tall grasses, they looked out across the view of the crisscross walls and the lime-green humps, they picked mushrooms in the mornings or watched the swallows swooping at the end of the day.

Of Nathaniel, they saw little – he would be out gathering wood or walking up in the top forest or down on the far beaches – but this did not deter the stream of visitors who ventured to the edge of his mountain to sup the sweet wine of celebration that seemed to hang in the golden air.

In the valley also, Megan could remember that the atmosphere of contentment was tangible. On Sunday mornings, you went to church and the people were there, sat in serried ranks, hats on, gloves folded flat across their knees, proud, everyone, proud to be in their church on their Sundays.

For Father Duncan, in these days, sermons came easily. The words in the Bible had meaning, were clear, all the stories enlightening and the message not a dogma but an essential truth. For Shiny Blackford, God was good because Megan was his once more – not in the way that he had envisaged but at least now he could visit her, be with her, they could talk about things as though it were a life shared.

For Megan herself, God was good because he had by that time dimmed the hateful memories and saved her from the burden of her son. For the Hotblacks and the Clothiers, the Joneses, the Jessops, the villagers and farmers, these times did not seem to bring the failing crops, the empty market stalls, the sickening children that they remembered from before.

In these golden, sainted times, God was! And they all –

the villagers, the farmers, Megan Capity, Father Duncan –
they all attributed their blessings to the day when he rode
through their table-lined lane, the day when they were first
joined by Nathaniel Cadwallader.

Part Three

One

Father Duncan saw them first. He was walking out along the top ridge when he noticed in the far distance a huddle of specks moving along the lane. Father Duncan had been humming to himself. He was thinking about the words that he would say, tomorrow, Michaelmas. He was thinking about the hymns that he would choose, the psalms, about the sermon. He was thinking that, with the coming of winter, he must clear the sacristy of the old cassocks, that he must ask Bessie to reblack the grate, that he must make sure there were plenty of logs in the store.

The way they moved, the way they were, the shape and size of them were perplexing to Father Duncan – they must be strangers. Father Duncan cut short his musings, watched as this weary group tripped along the lane heading for the valley. He wondered what it was that brought them there.

Later that day, Father Duncan called in at the tavern, asked the assembled drinkers about the strangers. The vicar described them, one tall, broad, one smaller, wiry, a third willowy. He told Duddon and Reilly and the others that the strangers looked poor, worn out. They must have passed through the village, he said, for when he had seen them, they were heading straight there. But no one had seen them and the Father's questions were met with blank faces.

On his way back to the church, Father Duncan stopped by at the bothy and asked Megan had she not caught sight of them while she was out minding the goats? But Megan had no recollection of seeing anyone, not unless you count the Old Man, that is, flopped in his chair, she said. Father Duncan was perplexed. Perhaps he had been mistaken. He thought no more of it.

A month or so earlier, Lysander Merritt had died. Bethan Clothier found him when she was rolling down the hill on her way home from the top paddock. He had been standing near a field gate towards the south-west of the village, leaning on a stick, chewing on some tobacco, bathing in that special sunshine that comes when the air is cold and the nights drawing in. Bethan found him and you could see he had been caught unawares. There was a look of surprise about him, not fear not pain but his eyebrows were up and in the rictus of his lips you could detect half horror, half smile. Bethan lifted his cap and placed it over his eyes. She replaced his stick in his hand, wiped the smear of tobacco from his chin, then made her way back to the village, no hurry, to tell the men so's they could come and load him on to Duddon's wagon.

He was not a great loss to the village, Lysander Merritt – just one of the thin layers of its fabric which gradually peeled away. Of course, everyone went to his funeral, modest though it was: Old Man Penhaligon, possibly the closest Lysander had come to a friend, placed there at the front of the church, head lolling, a trickle of spittle running from his mouth; Mary Jessop sniffing into her handkerchief; Duddon and Reilly and Nib sitting tall, sober in their Sunday best. But Father Duncan's address was short and soon the chorus of sniffs began to fade as the dry dirt rained down on Lysander's last glimpse of the sky.

No one gave much thought to Lysander's cottage now that it was empty. They left it well alone like you do when you are not really sad or glad and slowly, slowly the cobwebs joined hands across the windows and doors, dust gathered like a carpet of vultures, the mice who had always enjoyed the run of the place hibernated in the middle of the rooms, no shame at all. One or two roof tiles fell off in those September winds, a shutter hung precariously from its hinges. But to all intents and purposes, the place looked the same, the garden a wilderness, the cottage ramshackle.

He was always among them, Lysander Merritt. He was always there and he was crusty and crabbed and you could count on him for dry comment or a bark of disapproval. He was always there and they took him for granted but in truth, they knew little of him.

In fact, all of his life Lysander was a hoarder, collected nuts, acorns, boxes, straw. Pine cones, too, nests, wild flowers which he pressed, old sheep horns. If you peered in through the murk-dark windows of his cottage, you could see it all, the stacks and stacks of this, that and the other which he had accumulated over a lifetime of solitude. It went from floor to ceiling throughout and as you moved from one window to the next, you could see there was barely any floor space. Even his bed was built up on straw and the corridors were lined with an inner skin of pine cones and most of the rooms appeared several feet smaller in diameter for the sheer, monstrous amount of forest debris.

More famously, Lysander made walking sticks. He collected ash saplings and there were always strips of wood, piles of straight rods leaning against walls and furniture, even blocking doorways and windows. The place was a haven for mice, for birds, for beetles and wood lice. Inside, a straitened labyrinth of the forest, peppered with thousands of mouse droppings, smelling of damp and lightless decay. And outside, a haphazard wooden structure enmeshed in a strangling mask of honeysuckle, cobwebs, mistletoe – so that you could barely detect its presence, so that it almost dissolved into the countryside that surrounded it.

But a few days after Father Duncan had been out on his walk and seen the trio of strangers, Bessie came panting into Megan's parlour saying there's a fire, a fire, gasping, up at Lysander's old place, smoke, thick smoke, everywhere. The two of them ran out to his cottage, found a huge bonfire taking place in the garden, no one apparently about, just piles of horn and moss and twigs smouldering on a heap.

They did not know what to make of it. Someone had tried to cut down the weeds, to make some sense of the garden. The windows had been cut free, cleaned. A broom-head had been fixed roughly to some pole and run loosely across the porch floor. Through the darkness of the gaping door, Megan thought she could see the silhouette of a man but she could not be sure.

And a week after that, Shiny was out on the fell, mending a wall. The curlews were going, the swallows had gone and the sharp autumn sun bowed long and deep over the back of the purple sea. Shiny rubbed his hands over the front of his shirt to wipe the powder from his drying fingers. He thought I'll have a drink at the tavern and he turned to walk down the fell and he came through the trees, scuffed his heels in the early fallen leaves that crisped beneath him. All around him, wreaths of the brilliant colours of summer's death and Shiny breathed in, let the air run down to the depths of his lungs and he thought no I'll walk on, he thought, I'll go to Lysander's cottage, I will, I'll go and see the old place.

And he came round the corner and he saw all Lysander's ash saplings piled high on a pyre of sheep's heads and dead birds and round the flames, three of them – a woman, a man, a girl. And Shiny, who was both afraid and emboldened by his fear, he shouted out what do you think you are doing but they did not seem to care whether they were shouted at or not, only they kept their heads down, kept staring at the fire.

Later that night in the tavern, Shiny related what he had seen and the others they said they must be the ones as Father Duncan saw and at once they realised to a man that some strangers had come unbidden to live among them and they looked at one another and a tremor ran through them.

Two

Years later, when the tight ball of the village was unravel-
ling itself, when most of them were going or gone and
all who remained were Megan with her blind eyes and her
turning chair and Martha of Morland slowly packing, slowly
preparing to leave, Megan tried to sift from the woman's
ramblings and her dark brown I-told-you-sos the story of
their coming.

She said they had come far from here, from the plain
that ran to the east and the south of the valley. Winds
beat the plain like they beat the rocks on the open sea.
For as far as a man could see, there was barrenness, she
said. For as long as you could bear to stand up in it, the
winds beat and beat beyond. No birds, no peace, the sun
when it came only hot and hard. Close your eyes, feel
the burn of the wind, feel the empty and the bleak, she
said. Shot through with the pierce of the heat, the cold,
she said. Forsaken by birds, she said, no trees, she said,
forsaken by God.

Yet in the very centre of the barren, beaten emptiness,
a small house with a few empty, flapping barns besides.
Smoke puffing out of the chimney. And shuffling through
dirt-scraped earth, Martha of Morland herself, tall, broad,

heavy, her shoulders pulled down, her breasts hanging large, her belly bulging.

They were drawn, she said, by the space, drawn to the plain as a blind man would be to music. It was the cry to them of water in a desert. They had been born with nothing and then they had a chance to have something and it was this. There was a stream close by, the place had barns – there are four rooms, Isaac, what more could we ask for? All his childhood, she said, he had dreamt of some space of his own. All his childhood, he had longed for the feel of dirt beneath his fingernails, the chance to rear a cow or two, some sheep. Martha had watched as Isaac gazed at the land, at the view, at the open fields, at the clenched knot of his fist, the sweated coins wrapped within. Then she saw as Isaac closed his eyes, opened his hand to the man with the papers, signed with an X, walked out on to the plain.

Oh God but the summers were hard – from April until October, the sun beat down, no sign of a rain cloud. Martha and Isaac grew bowed to the winds, burnt in the everlasting heat. Isaac discovered that cows were exhausting, demanding, expensive to feed. He found that sheep died for no reason, that they let him down when he could least afford it, that his stock did not seem to care whether or not he talked to them by name, only bayed for more water, more feed. He found that the land was greedy, cheating, took his every ounce of strength, yielded only failure in return.

Martha discovered that Isaac in his disappointment gave up, sat down, took to staring morosely out across the plain, shut his ears to the noise of the cows and the sheep, shut

116

his eyes to the falling barns and the broken well, gave up, left her to do the work, which was more than enough for a woman alone.

And then came this summer, two, three, four years after they arrived, a fire-breathing, eye-blinding, hair-searing summer and you were wedged in the jaws of a dragon and your hair stuck to your head, your arms to their sides, your thighs to each other. Martha had no strength – she was pregnant – and she carried not one but two children, she knew it was two because at night when she tried to sleep and the heat was pressing her down into the pool of sweat that she had made beneath her, she could feel the tiptoes of too many feet against her ribs.

She knew that she carried two children but she could not rest, she said. There were jobs to do, could not sit down, stock to feed, to water, to tend, to graze. She dared not take the weight off her feet for fear that the day would be gone only to be replaced by another longer, drier, hotter. Martha was exhausted, dragged herself along in the dust. Dirt caked her mouth, the back of her throat and every day she climbed from her bed, hoping – oh God how she hoped – that the sky that greeted her would be black, smell of rain, that Isaac would be up before her, would have fed the cattle, watered the crops, done the chores.

But the days wore on and Isaac stayed in his chair and nothing she could do, no amount of hope or despair, no amount of hard work or rest or gut-tearing yells seemed to change anything, anything at all. In her evening prayers, she begged for rain and she begged for cool and she begged above all that her children would be two sons who would help her, work with her, save her from ever having to endure such misery again.

Then at last Martha's time came. She was in a state of delirium. Muttering on, lumbering on, not stopping, not for the pain, not for the clench or the jerk or the bite. Buckets in both hands, hay in her hair and this dreadful scream inside of her which was growing and growing and though she tried, God knows she tried, to make it all work, make time wait, feed the cows, fetch the water, soon she found herself flat to the dirt, water, hay, dust, pain, crying baby.

For an age, she lay there. Sucked out. Drained and filled and hot and frozen and waiting for the next one which she knew must surely come. At last Isaac was there and he saw her lying, dead almost and he saw the baby and he did not know what to do, she says, because Isaac never knew what to do, it was always her, what should I do, Martha, what should I do, my heart and he stood up, sat down, kneeled, wrung his hands, touched her head, shrank back. He went to pick up the child, to nurse it in his arms, she said, he went to walk away out of the barn, not thinking, not seeing that she was not finished, not even remembering what all summer they had carried in their minds as a dreadful knowledge, that there were two, not one but two. So Martha summoned up the strength she had, she said, the little strength and she croaked don't forget, Isaac, there's another, Isaac, pull it out.

And Isaac came back and he put down the baby and he got down on his knees and he pulled it out. And it was a boy. And it was dead.

Near-death exhausted, Martha on the hay-barn floor. Beside her, one bleating girl; one silent boy. There were no words, she said, no tears. There was nothing that Isaac could say or Martha could do and the world shut down, for one brief moment the winds ceased to howl as the pair

118

of them contemplated the living and the dead. He would never understand, she said, how much she had done for him. He would never understand.

On a wind-parched plain, in a hay-strewn barn, during the hottest summer in memory, Myfanwy of Morland was born.

He made a good mother, she said. For all of his dithering, for all of his bone-dead laziness, he looked after the girl from the start, she said, because she would have nothing to do with her, because it had all been just too damn much. He was tender, she said, and patient. All that time, she supposed, that he liked to spend on his animals and now here it was and he could spend it on his girl. Because you see, she said, all he knew were his cursed animals – sheep, cattle, chickens, horses, goats, cats, dogs, rabbits, foxes, badgers, any bird you could name. All he knew was taming them, talking with them, mending them, blowing soft old secrets from years on the land up their noses, down their beaks, in their eyes. When he held a hedgehog in his broad, wooden hands, when he poured a few drops of water into its gaping mouth, when by sheer stone-old stubbornness he nursed it back to life and set it free; when he helped the old mare to deliver her foal and the foal was tiny and crook-legged and he picked it up in his arms and took it into the house until it was warm, because the old mare was too exhausted, too worn-out to lick it free; when he went down on his knees, at the side of the mare and she's hot now, frothing and he touched her on her neck, soft into her muscle until the tightness went, until the heaving left her and the agony and she was free to die without the pain, without the fear – then, Martha said, Isaac was content, Isaac knew what to do.

And so it was with the girl, she said, like he had found her broken-winged, club-footed, half-blind. So he brought her into life, she said, with his simple, stupid kindness. He fed her, he bathed her, he loved her, he clothed her, he even named her, she said – for Martha did not care, did not even have the will to look at her, child that had killed her only son, child that had caused her nothing but grief.

And Myfanwy, who was only indulged by her father, who was not taught or guided, only spoilt and petted and allowed to run free because that was what he was like, Isaac, lazy, Myfanwy grew quick, sharp-eyed, fickle, sly. She was a careless waif, child that had been reared more like a calf or a feral cat, child that was free. Wild and beautiful and free.

The passing years were marked by cows that came and went, dogs that lived and died, crops that were sown, then wilted. As the girl grew up, she got wilder, Martha said, bonnier, fair enough, but wilder. Martha had no time for the girl. Martha cooked and Martha worked and Martha waited for the time when a son would come. Sometimes she sat and spoke a word to Isaac – sometimes she felt that old flame that once had melted them together all those years before. But mostly they just worked, moved through their own circles, barely touched.

And Megan, as she sat there in her warm-wood chair, trying to understand it all, she pictured a small tumbledown house and a large empty plain and three individuals, curious, uneasy. She saw some thin cattle, some ragged sheep, a stream that ran, thank the Lord, come hail or shine. And the picture rolls by always to the moan of the wind, the dole of the plain.

Then one day, sixteen years after that dreadful summer,

God sent down another scorching heatwave and this time, Martha of Morland was too old. She could not keep up with the needs of the cows and Isaac was too downhearted to be of any use and even between them they could not manage the kegs of water as they used to. They were forced to leave their wooden house and their barn and their brown dead land that was littered with the bodies of cows and sheep that had died from hunger and thirst.

Martha packs up and she leaves. Her rugged beauty, their dreams have gone. She has no son, she does not love her husband so much now, he has never worked as she has worked, she says they must leave and they leave. Martha says we must leave and Isaac packs a bag for Myfanwy, picks up an old fork that has always been his favourite, turns away from his dead home and his dead friends. And he walks because Martha says they must walk.

So they walked numbly through days of strangeness and exhaustion and fear, Martha and Isaac and Myfanwy of Morland, the tall, the wiry, the willowy. They left the parched plain, walked through hills and dales they did not see, walked and walked and walked away from their life's work until they could not walk any longer.

Three

During their first weeks in the village, Martha fills the gaps left by her pain with work, with clearing out Lysander's cottage so they can all have somewhere to lie down and weep quietly. She counts out the acorns, the birds' nests, the sheep skulls – ten, eleven, twelve – as though her loud, gritty enunciation of the numbers would keep the memories out. Then she puts them in buckets – a hundred and four, a hundred and five, a hundred and six – and transports them to the bonfire.

Isaac finds a stone, under the window with the mistletoe and he props his fork against the wall, sits down on the stone. He ignores the sounds of his wife as she grinds her way through the innards of this hovel they have landed in. He ignores the sun that is kind and the vegetation that is green and the flowers that are not burnt-brown but peep through long lush grasses and they are smiling. Isaac is too tired. He is too disappointed. You would almost say that nothing has changed.

So they do not notice when she goes, when she gives up helping, when she stops dragging out the rubbish, all the

123

feathers, stones, bits of the forest but skips off, leaving them as though it did not matter.

Myfanwy is sixteen. She is just sixteen. Yet for all that she has come from a different place, for all that has happened to her, for all that everything that she has known thus far has changed beyond recognition, this girl is bursting with life. You cannot help but turn your head when you see her. You cannot help but let your heart lift when you hear her sing. You feel her joy in her looks, in the drift of her green eyes and the swoop of her hair, in the fey shimmer of her as she goes from here to there and she does not care who looks and who does not.

Myfanwy runs through the woods, she runs up the hills, she runs as far as the sea – further than any other villager has ever been – and she dips her toes into the lilac waves just to see how it is to be surrounded by water, to be damp and cool after the hellish hot summer she has left. She might pick up an acorn and plant it, pick up another and do the same, pick up another and another and another until she has planted a forest – and all this on a whim, because something has caught her eye and she has thought I will do that. She might walk along with her hands waving by her sides to beat the grass as it leans over to have a touch of her veily cloak. She might rise at dawn, sleep in the winter sun, sit awake through the dark, through the sultry progress of midnight. She might see a bird and chase it, see a fox and throw a stick, then laugh with her head back and her hair running down the length of her dress.

Myfanwy is a poem, she is a lilting free-fall sonnet, an ode to beauty, to love, to the trees and the birds and the winds that float out across the mountains.

And today, she is heading down towards the woods that lead to the Penhaligon farm. Today, winter is here, has caressed the land with her diamond beauty, shines out from the tips of the grass and the leaves, from the branchy fingers of the junipers and the cones on the pines and Myfanwy is walking and Myfanwy is humming. And she picks up a stone and she throws it high, high in the air, lets her head back, opens her throat to the sky and she is a child, free and fair and she watches the stone as it arcs through the dark-soft blue . . .

. . . and Nib Penhaligon, who is standing in his yard, he sees her, sees her abandon and the line of her neck and the hair that drops down her dress and the lightness of her and Nib steps out so that she sees him . . .

. . . and Myfanwy forgets the stone, interrupts her tune, in that one instant sheds every last vestige of her childhood . . .

. . . because she sees how he looks, because she sees for the first time how a man looks at her, because she sees that Nib is pale and reddened, hot and chilled and all at once Myfanwy knows what it is that she is, what it is that she can do. She is a woman. A siren. She feels his yearning, even from here. She feels his surprise and his shock and his joy and his pain. She feels his greed and his fear, all this in an eye-blink and as she does so, Myfanwy smiles. Instinct bubbles up. She is a woman.

And Myfanwy returns his look – bold, sure, narcotic – from beneath the canopy of velvet lashes.

She looks at him and Nib Penhaligon is the first of all the men who falls within the magic of her spell. Nib Penhaligon who is rabbit-shy. Nib Penhaligon who never thought to find a single person who might care for him. Nib Penhaligon who is gauche with his hands and crude with his words.

Now she is no longer a child. And she draws him down

to the ice carpet of the forest moss and she sings him a song that he has never heard before.

For weeks, while her parents remain in the cottage eking out some kind of paupers' existence, hiding through loss and bad memories and broken spirits, Myfanwy amuses herself with Nib. Explores the reach of her powers, how she can tease him, toy with him. Like a cat with a mouse and she talks to Nib, she goes to his house – at dawn, in the middle of the night, whenever it takes her fancy – and she drives the boy insane with her push-me-pull-you, with her giving and not giving. She says I-will-I-won't. She says I-do-I-don't. She dances for him, she laughs for him, she shows him the words to her songs – or she is cold for him, she sulks for him and then she is not there when she has promised and Nib is broken-hearted.

And finally she tires of Nib because she has learnt from him all she can and Myfanwy turns to someone else, this time Bertie Hotblack, who is younger but he is not so shy and he knows a thing or two and now she is stretched a little, her ingenuity, her fickleness, her light cruelty moving to new levels as she seeks to leave him, like the unhappy Nib, all wrung out.

And then she tries it on the others, on Duddon and Reilly, on one of the Jones boys and one of the Cartwrights – even on Archie Jessop, who is a married man, who is a good deal older – because now that is who she is: she is the girl whom they all want, the girl who will and will not be had.

And they all succumb, every last one, to her waterfall-hair and her mermaid-eyes and her veils and the softness of her fingers and the way she knows now, just knows, what it is that they want. She does it because she can, she does it because she has never before had anything or anyone, she does it because it is her whim and she adores her whims. One by one, she picks them off. One by one, they fall for Myfanwy of Morland's incredible powers of seduction.

Word gets round about her. Of course it is only the women because the men are too hurt or too ashamed or still a little in love with her and so it is only the likes of Bessie and Bethan but in quiet moments, when they are sure they are not overheard – she has this way of just appearing, she does – they say words like slut and harlot and she-devil. And when they can, when they see her, which is not often, they shun her and they do their best to make their eyes burn hot and their shoulders look disgusted.

Soon, rumour turns on the parents and says they too are here only to make mischief. The fact that they move in without asking; the fact that they burn all Lysander's sticks when he had spent a lifetime collecting them; the fact that they do not come to church, that they do not say hello or even introduce themselves to the village, only they sit there all day long, staring at the ground; the fact that they let her do as she likes, let her come and go, leave the valley, come back to the valley as though it were just as easy as all that; all these add up to something that the villagers do not like because they do not like strangers, because they do not care for their times with Nathaniel Cadwallader to be interrupted.

But Myfanwy does not care for what they say or how they are towards her, all she cares for is her game, this new game that she has discovered, that she knows is hers, absolutely hers. She does not go home, she does not see Martha or

Isaac, only she drifts from one sublime encounter to the next, from one hapless man to the next.

Finally, as she must, Myfanwy runs out of men. No more new conquests. No more villager hearts to break because they are all – with the possible exception of Tom Sebley, whom she avoids, and Father Duncan, whom she never meets, and Shiny Blackford, who is not remotely interested – they are all broken. Minutes ago, she was new to all of this, she was a child, she had never known a man other than her father. But here, even so soon, she grows restless and bored – the villagers have been too quick, too easy.

Years later, when her chair is her nest and she has time to recall the detail, Megan remembers how here during that winter the seeds of change and ultimately disaster are sown. The men are disturbed, the women disgusted, jealous, rattled. Because Myfanwy is unnerving, her presence unsettling. Because somehow she is a mirror and when she holds it up to them, they see more than they care to know.

On a market day, it is late and they have tidied up but Bessie Hotblack is still there chatting with Bethan. Their twin buttocks are perched on the fountain – they do not know she is there, running her hand up, down along the buttresses of the church – and they are talking about Nathaniel Cadwallader. Bessie would rather die than let Myfanwy in on their secret. She has no time for Myfanwy, not for her pretty ways nor for her ribbons and tassels and she is furious with her too because she has some idea that the girl has played a part in why Bertie is so tetchy and ill-tempered. But Bessie does not know she is there in the shadows, listening.

And Myfanwy, who has never heard this man's name mentioned before, she pricks up her ears. She hears the reverence in their voices and her interest is piqued. She wonders who he is, this Nathaniel. Why has he not been to see her? Why has she not heard of him till now? But Myfanwy does not waste too much time wondering, only she gathers herself up, veils and all, tiptoes out from the graveyard, makes her way to the hill where she heard them say he lives.

Four

In this citrus-green valley with its year-long winds, through the shifting skies and the changing seasons, above the village, above the five-mile hedge, above the farmers as they work and the farmers as they rest, above the sounds of the sea and the cracks of the trees as now and again they fall in the woods, on the plateau of the hill in the tiny wooden chapel which the villagers worked so hard to restore, Nathaniel Cadwallader sits at his wood-carving bench.

He is at work on a talisman for Father Duncan – it is The Word. Of all the people in the valley, Father Duncan is one of the last to receive a carving from Nathaniel Cadwallader. It has no particular shape nor substance but The Word is minute in its detail and exquisite in its craftsmanship. Somehow, you know that it signifies The Word, The Word that is God. Perhaps, above all, this is Nathaniel's single greatest creation. Perhaps, above all, were you able to study this carving, you would understand about Nathaniel Cadwallader.

He is not a conscious artist. He is not a brilliant man, a planner, a strategist who says today I will carve this, today I will create this. You see his art and you see the work of a man who is part craftsman, part painter, part poet. You see a man who has been chosen by his work. He is instinctive, natural, has a feel for the wood that is extraordinary. You see his art and you see something that ought to be, something whose existence makes complete sense. You watch his hands as they glide across the table and you see confidence, sureness. You watch his fingers as they turn the wood and they do not let it slip, not even when his chisel is scraping hard or he is using a spike to pierce it through. You hear his breathing and there is no pause, no tension, only the easy rhythm of a man who is following his reason.

And in the shell-fragile beauty of the small, shining piece of wood that Nathaniel holds between his fingers, you can see the very spirit of the woodcarver's genius. Slowly, slowly he turns a rock into a jewel. The Word matures, emerges from the darkness of its smooth dark womb. The Word, the fusion of all ideas and all dreams and all faith, the fusion of all the doubts and hopes and fears and joys of Father Duncan and those like him who seek to be men-of-God. And Nathaniel Cadwallader, carving out the shadow of a man, the essence of a faith, the story of one whole glorious world, in some immeasurable way giving the man all the feelings, imbuing the faith with all its facets, imparting upon this tiny wooden ingot a whole story and a whole understanding which is far, far beyond Nathaniel himself.

Through Nathaniel's doorway, the light is streaming in. There is a fat ray that comes through the door and thousands of wafers of gleam that pour through the cracks in the wood and the gaps between the rough-hewn boarding of his workshed. Nathaniel's head is down, intent on the task in hand. He seems engrossed in his project, engrossed in the minute detail of The Word. His hands may be big but they are dexterous, nimble, adept at manipulating the tiny tools that he uses to refine this, his most intricate work of art.

All of a sudden, the body of his light is blocked. A shadow comes over. It is she, Myfanwy of Morland. She has come to see Nathaniel Cadwallader. She approaches the door and she stands within its frame and she looks at the man deep in his work.

Her shadow is stealing his light, disturbing the train of his thoughts and Nathaniel looks up. The gently, carefully, minutely polished talisman falls from his hand, plops on to the bench. The tools slide from his fingers, words melt into the air unsaid. Through the gaps in the boarding, the sun beats on Nathaniel's eyebrows, on the tip of his nose while the specks of dust that fall in the light feather his forearms.

She does not step back out of the light. She does not move from the doorway, returns unstintingly the gaze that is cast over her by the woodcarver. No words, not one, not a breath, not a harrumph, not a cough but the light is still and the air is still and Myfanwy is fixed, rock-set to the floor. For a moment, the birds outside that were singing and the horses in the field that were flicking their tails and chomping and the farmers below that were raising their scythes and thrashing the grass – for a moment, all these cease to move, to breathe, to be for it is only Nathaniel and the girl, the one transfixed by the other. For many minutes, hours, days even, they remain thus, the sun lightening the dark cascade of her hair, eyes and heart and soul stricken with new sensation.

Then, slowly, slowly the breath comes back and the flecks of dust that were suspended above Nathaniel's arms resume their meandering descent; slowly Nathaniel's frozen person melts and he sees the dropped talisman and the scattered tools and he resumes his position at his bench, his head bent over, his shoulders and back and arms fixed on his work.

She says nothing, does not move. She watches him as he carves, as he hones and rubs and jostles the grain. Shaking hands, shaking heart and she watches the sun as it beams in around him while the chisel scrip-scrip-scrapes upon the wood and the flecks of dust keep falling, falling.

A few days later, Nathaniel goes out for a walk and Donald is there in his shadow and he sees how Nathaniel is – just wandering through the cornfield, crunching the stubble with his great boots, thoughtful. Donald walks behind him. Donald is swamped in silence, a silence that is fear and also maybe jealousy but definitely fear because he saw her when she came to the chapel and he could see what she was trying to do. And Donald may be slow and heavy but his instincts are sharp, he is quick to sense a change, quick to sniff out a threat and he does not know whether to say something, whether to do something, whether just to pray that it is nothing, that soon it will go away.

Fretful, disturbed, at nights he has not slept but lain awake in bed and listened to find out whether or not Nathaniel seems altered. And during the day also, Donald has been watchful, afraid, and he has tried to estimate whether or not there is a difference, whether or not Nathaniel works as he always has, whether or not he tends his mares, his stallion as he always has – but Donald cannot be sure. Is there a difference? Has the girl caught his eye? Donald is afraid and he allows his fears to grow because that is how he is, because Nathaniel is his rock and what would happen if that rock were to waver, because this has never happened before, no one has ever come up to Nathaniel Cadwallader like this.

Donald follows Nathaniel's gaze through the cornfield. He watches his eyes – first they are down, scouring the bald patches of earth between the cut stalks as though they might contain an answer; but then they are up. Nathaniel has seen something in the distance and Donald can see he is not sure what.

It is many-coloured, dazzling. It is the glow that you see in your eyes if you close them and face the sun. It is the colour that comes in the dreams that you have when you wake and you are warm. It is the colour of triumph and tragedy and joy. It is the colour that strong men carry in their eyes when they think of the wars they must win and the fears they must brave.

Donald must run to keep step with Nathaniel who is marching now, marching purposefully towards the source of all this colour. Ten, maybe twelve large strides he takes, he bounds, the strides of a man in seven-league boots, and he is there – the younger man sprinting in his wake – and Donald sees, they both see, that the colour is the colour of flowers, of a thousand, thousand flowers, of all the flowers in God's garden, all the flowers that were ever made in the kingdom of this earth – blues and reds, magentas and greens, vermilions and ochres and gentians, all the blacks and the greys, all the browns and the emeralds and the sapphires, all the jewels, all the large-petalled, scooped bowls, all the filigree, tiny-petalled, fragile blooms, not just a rainbow but the rainbow, not just a kaleidoscope but the kaleidoscope.

Nathaniel cocks his head and Donald hears, as Nathaniel hears, the swish of the wings of the butterflies who flit through the flowers as though they had always been here.

For now they are in the middle of the rainbow. And in the distance, they see a form and Donald knows that this is her, she is there, in the centre of her triumph, rising above the flowers, her head back, her throat open to the sky. She is twenty, maybe thirty feet above the ground, she is a goddess on a cloud and you know you will never see the like of this again.

In the shadow of his woodcarver friend, Donald stands and Donald watches. He sees Nathaniel Cadwallader as Myfanwy of Morland makes to seduce him – with her flowers and the turn of her neck and the deep golden-green canopy of her gaze. He smells the ineluctable tug of all that perfume. He sees, laid out before him, the multi-brilliant weavings of her scheme and Donald turns and Donald runs because now his fear is real, because now he must tell someone that she is trying to take him away.

Donald runs to the village. The first person he finds is Tom Sebley and he stutters it out in the mumbly-rumbly kind of way that he has, stutters it out about the girl and Nathaniel, about how she is doing it to him like she did it to Nib and Bertie and Archie and the others, because Donald saw it all, every last moment.

And Tom listens and he is not sure quite what the boy is getting at but he has an idea, he has a good idea.

When she was planning all this, dreaming up the snare of the field and the flowers and how she would lure him to her, Myfanwy pictured it all in her mind's eye. It was all mapped out and she could see him as he came and he saw her, as he came and he saw her work and he fell in love. She knew he would come because she chose a field that cut across his. She knew he would come because who would not, because it was all so bold, because who had ever resisted her before?

He would walk towards her, his face lit up by her rainbow. He would step right up to her and she would let him wait, for a moment, maybe two, long enough so that he would know that it was she who was in charge. And then at last when he had stood and trembled, when he had quaked in her presence, she would drift closer, draw him down, run her finger over the ridge of his back, cradle his head on her lap as her heart sang out let me be close to you, let me be near to you, let me hear your special story.

And they would sit there or they would lie there and all around it would be quiet and she would fill the silence with tales from her childhood. Come with me, Nathaniel, and she would show – with her arms, with her words, with her wispy ethereal gestures – she would show him the things that she loved on her farm, in her early youth, in the days when she spent so much time alone, free, wild.

Come with me, Nathaniel – and she would tell him of her secret places and her favourite haunts, of the trees that she knew and the caves and groves that she roamed and the dreams that she spun when she sat alone under a star-dark sky.

Come with me, Nathaniel, come with me, and she would take him to the farm and to the land that now is dead and abandoned but once was filled with Isaac's beloved creatures.

She would plant for him a field of a thousand, thousand flowers, she would rise, goddess on a cloud, she would lure him with the turn of her, with the bold of her, with her never-ending song – and then she would wait for him to fall, as they all had, fall under her spell, fall into her lap, fall upon his knees.

But it does not seem to happen that way; somehow, it does not.

Instead, it is Myfanwy herself who falls in love. Instead it is she, she who has never connected, who now finds herself in another's thrall.

For nights after her visit, Myfanwy does not sleep. She does not sleep, not at the cottage, not in the woods, not anywhere. Something has touched her. Something has reached down inside of her and Nib who is still dogging her steps, Bertie Hotblack whose eyes are still scouring the horizon for her shadow, they see her as she wanders from here to there, as she drifts about the valley and they know now, if they did not know before, that their chance to be loved by Myfanwy of Morland has gone. She is, if not possessed, at least disturbed.

Myfanwy feels the tables of her demons turn for now it is she who is all wrung out, she who lies awake at night plotting about how she may bump into him, how she may just happen to be out on the path that he is using for wood-gathering, how she may just happen to look tearful or divinely radiant or something, something so that she can capture his heart as he has surely captured hers.

Myfanwy is in love and she racks her brains for plans and stratagems by which she might win over her Nathaniel Cadwallader. She walks the forests looking for pieces of wood to bring him for his work; she appears at the chapel with bunches of flowers or garlands of berries; she offers to help Donald with the horses, tend the foals, check the water – but there is no joy in all of this, Donald will not speak to her, Nathaniel is either absent or else he does not respond in the way she hopes and soon Myfanwy is not just lightly in love but tearfully, passionately.

Myfanwy is in love and the object of her desires seems to her at least unmoved. There seems to be no change in him at all. Even after the field of flowers, even though he saw her there and she had done all she could to paint the sky as a sainted iridescent backdrop to her beauty, even then there is no difference. He does not seek her. He does not smile at her or ask to touch her. He does not give her any sign, none at all, only when she bars his path he looks at her, and she does not know how to interpret his look and she falls further and further.

At last, she goes to her mother, for the first time in her life Myfanwy of Morland goes to her mother and she asks Martha what she is to do, how she is to win over Nathaniel Cadwallader. She asks her, she pleads with her, she begs from her any tricks she might have – and she waits, with her head and her hands on the ground in the weed-strangled garden of Lysander Merritt's old cottage, she waits for Martha's answer. But it is too late for Myfanwy and Martha, too late because Isaac is dying and Martha is all caught up in nursing him, in contemplating the calamitous picture of their time together and besides, Martha has no answers because she herself never had any guile, only brute determination.

How can she do it? How can she make him love her? How can she make him see that it must be, that they must be, that she is no more than a missing part of him?

And then when she is all but in despair, Myfanwy has one last idea – a brilliant, brave idea. She will prepare a feast! She will invite all the villagers. There will be a grand celebration and she will be there, goddess on a cloud, and he will see her – centre of this triumph – and he will love her as she knows she must be loved.

She will wear a dress that has been woven from cobwebs and diamond dust – pink it will be, pink like God's kiss of the morning sun when day is almost dawned, pink like the fragile tinge of a wild rose, pink but silver, pink but diamond, pink but so frail, so feathery that she will seem to be wearing flamingo down. In her hair, she will wear floating ribbons, crushed rose petals, scents from all the blooms that she has sown in the top meadow. She will sprinkle powder of dreams in her hair, powder that she has made from pearls and shells and dandelion seeds and all her deepest, fairest love.

And in the middle of it all, at the height of all that jubilation, when he is there and she is there, when all the villagers are around and all the food is piled high on their plates, she will walk towards him, she will ask for silence, she will ask them to raise their cups, she will ask him in front of them all to marry her.

And Father Duncan, he will bless them, he will marry them and all the villagers who witness this spectacle, they will rejoice, at last, sing out, at last, be kind to her, generous, well-disposed at last towards her because it has been a grand day, because she has done a good thing, because their union is blessed and this is what was always meant to be.

In her visits to Nathaniel's chapel, Myfanwy has noticed the piles of coins that are stacked here and there, scattered about the floor. She has noticed how Nathaniel's mattress is unnaturally raised from the bed so that it almost touches the eaves for all the hordes of coins that Nathaniel has stowed beneath.

This is the money that Nathaniel receives from the farmers each time a mare is served by Dungarry. Myfanwy will take the money! She will go and ask plate-makers to make golden plates, glassmakers to carve golden chalices, linen-makers to weave sheets of white with threads of gold. She will go and whisper to the bees to pollinate all the flowers, to change the lilies, the snowdrops, the almond blossom, the daisies, the narcissi, the jasmines from white into gold. She will go and ask the seagulls, the doves, the swans and geese to hide for just one day their white feathers and to fly to this great feast in down that is golden. She will ask the insects, all the flies and wasps and bees and butterflies to dress in gold, to flutter in the breezes so that you are sitting there at this great feast, perched on the top of the long ridge, and everywhere there is white or there is gold and you would think that the bees and the flies were not insects but drops of rain, drops of golden rain waiting to fall upon the God-blessed couple.

Boars, lambs, calves, geese, swallows' eggs and ostrich hearts, the fruit of the vine, the tree, the bush, the hedgerow, the forest floor will be massed on plates, piled high until you are afraid that if you shift your chair or sneeze or laugh, the top morsels will tumble down the sides of the ridge into the valley-rifts below.

There will be flowers, there will be horses, there will be plates of gold and ribbons of gold. With her own hands, she will bake and cook and roast and boil and, most important of all, she will brew the wine – from the blossom of flowers and the nectar of bees, from the sap of this fruit and that tree and then she will arrange a fountain that soars up between the tables of food, a fountain that is never-ending, whose jet is as high as the knife-sharp hills beyond. Its golden spray will arc to the clouds, intoxicate the birds and insects who are hanging in the air, seduce the guests, their children, and above all help her to win his heart. Everyone will come. It will be the greatest feast, the best of times.

Such is the beauty of her plans, such is the strength of the love of Myfanwy of Morland for the woodcarver, Nathaniel Cadwallader.

Myfanwy goes about her schemes – seeks out linen-weavers here and candle-makers there, cajoles with her flatteries and wheedles with her guile and begs with her money – and there is no one in the village who knows what is afoot. No one, least of all Nathaniel Cadwallader himself, has an idea of her plans for the wedding.

But after church, in the tavern, in the market square, an atmosphere is building. All the words about Myfanwy and her family begin to join together. They begin to build up into a climate of discontent and alarm. There is something about her that makes the villagers afraid. For sure, she is fair. And aye, she is captivating and her eyes are beautiful and, of course, she should be allowed to fall in love and, yes, in many respects, she is a credit to the valley.

But the way she goes about it, the way she walks straight up to him while they always keep their distance, the way she knows even without knowing just what it is that will turn men's nights into sleepless encounters with hell, the way she does not allow anyone or anything to deflect her – all these elements combine to bring the first hint of unease since all those twenty years ago when he came among them.

And though they cannot articulate their fears, they are

afraid and it is a gut fear and it takes hold of their loins and it is both something and nothing, both justifiable and groundless.

So as she wafts about the village with a skip in her step and a song in her throat, with a thousand beautiful plans swarming through her head, there are almost as many eyes that follow in her wake. Eyes peeping out from behind twitching curtains. Eyes that are suspicious. Eyes that do not trust.

Father Duncan, at last he senses the shift in the atmosphere. He has scarcely seen the girl but he has heard how lovely she is and how bewitching. And he has heard how she spends all that time up on Nathaniel's hill, how she is barely away from the place and Father Duncan is afraid because he feels sure they must preserve Nathaniel, they must not lose him; without Nathaniel they return to the days before these golden times.

Shiny Blackford, he too is nervous of what will happen to Donald and then to Megan if Nathaniel is drawn away from them. Nib Penhaligon, he is torn between terror and joy – terror because she is the only one who has shown anything akin to love for him, joy because at last the temptress that she is might disappear.

Of course, there are plenty who do not feel so strongly about her: Duddon and Reilly, because every now and then, she comes to find them again, because every now and then, she takes them as she took them first and they are always ready, waiting; the boys Penhaligon, because though they were too amazed to fall in love with her, still they dream about her and they do not care whom she has known since or why, only they continue to fantasise about the time when they were hers; Archie Jessop, who cannot imagine what all the fuss is about, who took what there was as though it had been a piece of bread, who forgot about it the moment it passed his lips, who went about his days again as though nothing had ever happened.

And then there are the others, the ones like Old Man Penhaligon, who are too blind now, too old to see how she looks. Or the ones like Tom Sebley, who feel, after all this time, that here is a chance to overturn some injustices, that now that the girl is courting Nathaniel Cadwallader, maybe she will take him away and Tom will be able to reinstate himself as the rightful leader of the village, as the rightful hero of the valley like he was when he was younger, like he was before *his* coming. Tom Sebley rubs his hands together. He too can sense the shift in atmosphere, the suspicion, the jealousy and he is glad. He takes Myfanwy's velvet gaze into his dreams, only not for its beauty but for its danger. Surely he can use her?

But of all the villagers who have mixed feelings about the arrival of Myfanwy of Morland, Donald Capity is the most fearful of them all.

That moment when she held him with her green eyes, when she planted all those flowers, when she rose from a cloud and he saw her; those times when she comes to the hill and she stands in the doorway of his shed and she watches him work and she shows no shame in disturbing him; all those times when she is up in the woods and she thinks no one is looking and she is running one hand down her arm, fingers down her legs, preening herself – Donald has seen her, Donald has seen him see her.

And then there are other times – times when Donald

thinks Nathaniel is not sleeping, Nathaniel is not working so well, Nathaniel is careless with the stallion and a mare is kicked or a foal is put in needless danger; times when Nathaniel seems to have let go of Donald, seems to have taken his eye off the boy. Donald is afraid because Donald has no one else. Of course, there is Megan but she is not the same, she has never been the same as Nathaniel Cadwallader.

Then Donald follows Myfanwy and he finds her counting out to herself the coins that she has stolen from Nathaniel's shed and he hears her talking to herself about the wedding, about the feast and how he is going to love her and all Donald can feel is the terrible stab of betrayal. He knew it! In his ears, he feels burning. In his heart, he feels a gaping hole. His life is about to be pulled up by the roots and Nathaniel Cadwallader has not come to the boy, he has not placed his hand upon his shoulder, he has said nothing.

Mute, uncommunicating as a child, Donald shrivels up within his shell once more and from the fright of his retreat, he sees it all, sees how he will no longer be needed, how it will be Myfanwy who gathers the wood, holds Dungarry, leads the mares, feeds the foals. He sees Nathaniel Cadwallader as he comes up to Donald and asks him to leave. He hears Myfanwy of Morland as she comes up to Donald and orders him to leave. Nathaniel will not need Donald any longer. Nathaniel will not help Donald any more. Nathaniel will not love Donald, remember Donald, will cast him out . . .

. . . And Donald is afraid to wait until this time. He bubbles up inside himself, feels all the gases of jealousy pool in the back of his throat – and though he too has marvelled at Myfanwy's beauty, though he too has taken to bed fantasies of her golden-green eyes and her waterfall-hair, though he too has lain in bed at night with his great fists stuffed into his mouth that no one might hear the wails of lust and longing that rise up from his loins, Donald gathers himself up and once again, for the first time for more than a dozen years, he disappears.

Five

Yet today, there is a cheer in the air. Today, the Celtic pipes sound joyful, the hills and valley ring with their sounds. At last, her secret is out, she has told them her plans, she has asked them to come and today is the day. The winds are still and round the valley, there are sounds of preparations, of you-do-this and you-do-that, of put-on-this-no-that, of scrubbing of faces, shining of boots, primping of hair, tightening of stays. Voices of children, squealing, chattering. The women, high-pitched, chattering also. The men pretending that it is no concern of theirs, all the same as full of anticipation as any of the women and the children.

They have decided they will embrace the day. They have decided they will let their fears ride. Because they are greedy to know and see, because curiosity is harder to suppress than it is to indulge, because they have seen her food, they have smelt her wine, they have watched as the ridge has become laden with riches, because, after all, how many invitations in your lifetime do you receive to a feast and a day such as this?

So for all their suspicion of her, for all their fears and all their will to protect Nathaniel Cadwallader, they don their best. First the Clothiers – Bethan and Alfred, all the baby Clothiers. Hair is being marshalled – you can feel the scrape of comb on flesh. Fat, working muscles are squeezed into fine, unaccustomed wedding garb, tiny grubby arms and legs are scrubbed and slotted into trousers and dresses that are clean and scratchy, not at all comfortable. And the Hotblacks – Bessie is tittering, uneasy in her smart shoes; Albert stern and pompous by her side; Bertie by turns sullen, aroused, irritable. Then the Joneses, the Cartwrights, the Jessops – most look stiff in their dresses and suits but, for all that, their eyes shine.

Further along, the farm of the Penhaligons – the brothers are dressing, oafs in pantaloons, rubbing their hands together, making *AAAARGH* noises because they like drinking and they like feasting and this will be only the second time in their lives that they have been able to do both on any grand scale. Upstairs, Nib, pale, quiet, hiding in his starched shirt; in the yard, the Old Man, his chair polished, his chin wiped free of spittle, patient now.

Within the vaulted darkness of the church, Father Duncan, kneeling at the altar, finery in place, praying to the Lord Almighty for the strength to see this through, to make it right. She has asked him to bless them. She has asked him to marry them up there in front of them all. And Father Duncan is filled with nerves – he must not allow the twinges of alarm which he feels pulsing in his chest to colour his words.

Tom Sebley, whistling between his teeth, foxy, pulling a tie around his neck as though he was off to see his own girl, animated, calculating, waiting.

Only one or two do not join in all of this, one or two who cannot seem to put aside their fears, who cannot seem to see this day as good. Megan Capity standing before her mirror. She has picked bulrushes and broad red poppies which she plans to plant around the border of her hat, but her hat is on the chair and the flowers lie limp on the table. Megan stares at her image. She is dressing only slowly, only reluctantly and she cannot explain why it is so, why she is not skipping into her shoes as all the rest are, only she has a feeling, a distant nagging feeling and at first she cannot be sure, cannot pinpoint exactly what it means. She has an urge to see Donald, to go and see her son, an urge to step up the sponging hill, to pass through the gate in the five-mile hedge, to go and tip her hat at Nathaniel Cadwallader and just plain and simple reassure herself that all is well.

But now is not the time. Now, today, he too will be preparing himself, she is sure. Megan picks up her hat, drops it over her deep chestnut hair, picks up a poppy. She finds she is not deft as usual but clumsy, her fingers slipping. Why is it that she trembles so? Why is it that her stomach churns and her feet are leaden? Once again Megan wonders, just wonders if she should be doing this, here, now, if she shouldn't be going up the hill, just to have a word with Nathaniel to make sure that all is fine.

And lastly, in Lysander Merritt's old cottage, Isaac and Martha – father and mother of the bride. Martha, immobile in her wooden chair, her chin set, her sagging body clad in the same old rags. Beside her, Isaac, laid out on a bed in the front parlour, unable almost to see, far retreated into the darkness of his own impending death. Somewhere, in a cloud above him, memories of the farm he left behind, memories of the brown dead land and the scattered dead bodies of his cattle and sheep – but mostly there are no

149

memories for he is just tired now, wheezing breaths, limp arms, heavy heart.

She has not told them. God only knows why but Myfanwy has not told them about today. Maybe she is too excited, too naïve, too swallowed up in the fever of it all; maybe they did not love her enough or guide her when she needed it; or maybe she does not want them there because Martha at least would see through it all, might cause an unseemly moment during an otherwise joyous occasion; maybe it is possible maybe that she owes her father a debt and she does not want them to see him like this. God only knows.

Now there is a rumbling of drums, a trilling of pipes. Last-minute curses, wails of frustration die down in a welter of anticipation. The valley, the forest, the knife-sharp hills ring with whispers, fanfares, a slow chorus of gaiety and it builds up as she comes, as the centre of this, the grandest of days, draws into view.

Here she comes, here she comes! The children rush out into the lane, the birds flock to hang by the edges of the tree branches, the deer emerge from the spinney and stand at the top of the forest track. Foxes, badgers, otters, weasels leave their earths, their setts, their dams, their dens, converge on the edges of the hills and ridges so that all around, wherever you look, there are small heads, small eyes, big eyes, antlers, long ears fringing the horizon, low and high, like dominoes.

She is seated in a chariot that is drawn by Dungarry. Never in the memory of the villagers has this stallion looked more impressive and for a moment, the tunes and the drums are stifled by the *hurh* of gasps that rustles through the waiting lines. She is still, unaccompanied, does not smile.

150

Days, weeks, months later, the talk in the tavern, round the market square, in and out of the cottages is of how she appeared on that day, how legend-butterfly-heaven she looked in her fabulous gown, in her fabulous chariot drawn by the finest conker-brown stallion in the whole of the land. She was gold, gauzy gold and pink, dewdrop pink and it dripped from her hair and it laced through her fingers and it powdered into a perfect sprinkling mist that shrouded them all. There was a smell – of lilac and lily-of-the-valley, of stock and phlox, of roses and violets; and there was a song and the song sang out, so sweet that you could not help but smile, so loud that all the doubts of all the weeks that have led up to this day are drowned out and you sing along, and your ears and eyes and heart are filled with joy.

And now that she is here in all of her glory, they process to the top ridge, men, women, children, with scarves and ribbons and tails streaming out behind, to take part in the banquet which has been laid out on one long table that runs the length of the scar.

Years later, when she turns it over and over in her sightless mind, when she tries to recall the detail of that day, Megan finds that she cannot do so. It was all a blur, from the valley to the ridge, a blur of succulent, lavish, exotic food; of soft, loud, crooning, raucous song; of dancing that might have been slow and might have been so rowdy that the mountains jumped and the trees loosened their roots; a blur induced by fear that has been put to one side, by excitement, by the magic dust and the intoxication that flowed from Myfanwy's wine-fountain.

The only thing that Megan can clearly remember is the game that they played – in the middle of it all, in the midst of drinking and feasting, dancing, laughing, forgetting – when she stood up, Myfanwy, and she asked them to draw it for her, to record it for her, to take down every detail that they could. She wanted, she said, a history of it all. She wanted them to draw it as they saw it, to note down for her on the tablecloths before them all the things that they loved, all the food, all the people, Father Duncan in his vestments, Dungarry at the head of the chariot, Myfanwy herself in her dress of veils. This way, she said, you will give us a unique gift. This way, you will bring to us, to me, to Nathaniel, a picture, a kaleidoscope of how it was today, the grandest of days.

So drunkenly, eyes hazed and minds fuzzed, the Alfreds and the Bessies, the Shinys and the Archies and the Marys, they picked up the pencils which she had arranged in small pyramids about the tables and they swept the gold plates, the chalices, the knives and forks to the ground and they began to put it down, as they saw it, as she had asked.

Hesitantly at first because none of them was an artist, then less so, they arced and lined, circled and shaded and sketched. Some of them showed the village and the church, the dark dipping shadows of the cedar boughs, the ups, downs, flats of the graveyard headstones bobbing in a sea of wild flowers. Some of them chose to depict the valley itself in all its diversity, from the knife-sharp ridges to the low, soft drumlins, from the depth of the woods to the endless stretch of the sea. Many of the sketches were impressionistic, not only because they were not artists or they were intoxicated but because that was all it was to them, just an impression, not details but an atmosphere, not nuts and bolts but an edifice.

But others were bolder, more meticulous, and they recorded faces and postures, occasions, births, deaths, marriages. Tom Sebley – for even he joined in – he drew Donald as a boy, that time when they lost and then found him and he drew him sleeping, hair tousled, clothes scattered about the floor of his upstairs bedroom. Father Duncan tackled the interior of his beloved church, down to the stacks of leather-bound Bibles in the sacristy, down to the pews and the altar, the banner-laden beams, the gentle-tinted panes of glass in the great rose window. Megan Capity, by now far too carried away in the surge of the moment to dwell on her earlier anxieties, she drew the fell and the dry-stone wall, the scuffs in the dirt and a fallen stick, and as she completed it, you were not sure whether her face was clouded or not, whether she was glad or sad about all that had gone before.

They drew with a flourish, they drew in a frenzy, they drew until every last space on the tablecloths was covered. They drew until they could draw no more because all their ideas were spent, all their history was there for all to see – from his coming to the day of the wedding, from Donald's birth to Lysander's death and all the glorious days in between, all the sunshine hours and the sky-tall harvests, all the houses, all the faces, all the songs – and they drew because she asked them, for Myfanwy to pore over, for Myfanwy and Nathaniel to enjoy as this, the villagers' unique gift.

And as the game came to a close and the villagers' pencils ceased to dot up and down over the surface of the bright-white linen, still the food continued to come and more than that, her wine-fountain continued to pour – an endless cascade – and you stood with your cup beneath its honeyed arc and you drank the wine and you felt grand; you drank it and you loved whomsoever you saw. Now that their task was complete and the dancing had begun, the boys Penhaligon and Duddon and Reilly did not leave the fountain once. Mary Jessop took her golden chalice so many times that for once her handkerchief remained within the safety of her sleeve. Nib Penhaligon drank so much that, at one point, he was brave enough to invite the lovely bride to dance. Bethan and Bessie and even Megan herself became so overwhelmed by the joys of it that at some moment, you might have looked up from your conversation or your banqueting and you would have seen these women seated on the ground, their hair soaked in wine, their faces flushed and glistening.

No one cared on this day about any other. No one could imagine that this would ever come to an end. The fountain poured, wine golden, soft and it flowed from the vat like holy nectar. The fountain flowed on and on and the more they drank, the more beatific, joyous, loving they became. They drank to forget, they drank to indulge, they drank until they could not drink any more. The party continued for an endless year. It was a year that passed in a day. It was a year in which all the good feelings, all the release, all the frenzy of excitement which man can feel when he stretches out, when he reaches his arms to the sky, when he drinks and feasts and loves whomsoever he looks at, was condensed into one great, long day.

The fountain rose in a soaring golden arc, keeping them singing, keeping them smiling, keeping their feet tapping and their hearts dancing, as all the while, she sat in their midst, radiant as the dawn, high above, goddess on a cloud.

God breathes his dreams through Nathaniel Cadwallader! Today was the grandest of days.

*   *   *

And on that day, you could say she fulfilled her wildest dreams. For on that day, for all of that sainted day, every eye in the valley was fixed on Myfanwy. All the ears in the valley were focused on her song. Saturated with wine, replete with food, taxed by the game, intoxicated by the dancing, the joy, the Holy-Mary-Mother-of-God splendour of the whole occasion, the villagers had eyes only for her. No one thought to ask about anything other, to look for the groom, to see how he was, to scan his face for pride, for pleasure, for last-minute doubt. No one who was there – ask any of them – could remember how he seemed, was he glad, was he bold, was he proud, did he dance – such was the impression that Myfanwy of Morland, her entourage, her stately, other-worldly entrance made upon the people who first lined the lane, then traipsed up the hill, down the dale, up the other side to be seated at the white and golden ridge with the showers of birds and bees hovering on the winds.

It was as though Myfanwy's beauty, the fantasy of her plans eclipsed him altogether. It was as though the one person entirely absent from his own wedding was Nathaniel Cadwallader himself.

Who knows, perhaps he was not there, perhaps he stayed all day in the closet of his workshed, scraping and rubbing and chiselling at The Word? Perhaps he stayed behind in the cool of his work hoping that if he did not move, if he stayed and did what he always did, perhaps his young friend, his helpmate would sense it so and would return? Perhaps Nathaniel was always, had always been preoccupied with this foal, that carving, takes part in these celebrations only in spirit, only in the imaginations of those who would wish him to be there? Perhaps he is no more than a simple man, Nathaniel Cadwallader, no more than a woodcarver, no more than a parcel of hope upon whom others visit their dreams?

Part Four

One

The path that leads to the swanny-pool snakes its way up through the forest like a silver anaconda – in and out of the larch and hazel and alder that litter the lower reaches of the woods, round and through the upper forest, beyond the ridges, above the fells.

No one can see you climbing the path to the swanny-pool but on every step of your journey, you can look down on the valley that it shadows and you can hold in the small of your palm the Penhaligons and Sheepshankses working in the fields, Megan Capity walking behind her sheep and goats, the church, the tavern, the hub of the village.

After a while comes a fork in the path, barely distinguishable. You must go to the left, scuttle along a slithering, slanting track so covered with needles that it masks the sound of your footsteps. Now you are climbing into the clouds, through a glade that is drenched always with the mist and the dew of the dawn. Creepers reach down to touch your shoulders, squirrels scurry off to clear your way. Here is where no man comes, no man knows of. Here, at last before you, is the swanny-pool.

The water is blue as diamonds. You could pick up drops of it and lace them in your hair. You could dance across its glinting surface, you could clothe yourself in a robe of silver from its magic touch, you could count the lines on your face in its glass reflection. In the middle of the water, a large black rock juts up, sheer, and sometimes it is a glinting island and sometimes a lurking menace.

The swanny-pool is a place to worship, a place to dream, a place to bathe, to pray, to kiss the hand of God. In the best of times, on the best of days, there is a hanging haze and the water is blurred so that you cannot tell where the sky stops and the pool begins. All the bushes round it shimmer with drops and when a deer comes to drink or a fox, it seems as though in the whole world it is only you and they that exist.

On the best of days, it is purple and blue at the swanny-pool and you are up there, close to the sky and you are hugged in by the trees that bow over and there seems to be a whisper from every side and you could cling to your knees with your arms wrapped round and stay there all day long. On the best of days, you are there on your own, you are Megan Capity or you are Shiny Blackford and you do not know of another soul that is alive for the sky is clear and the air is flat, flat-calm and all you hear, in the far, far distance, are the bells of grazing goats or the soft moans of the wind.

But today, the path is no harbinger of peace and beauty. Today, the path is narrow and awkward, dew-soaked, slippery for the feet of the men who are struggling to carry something large back down its slopes. A pocketful of men – Tom Sebley, Shiny Blackford, Albert Hotblack, Reilly MacReilly – share a bundle between their aching shoulders. It is heavy, this bundle, and with a man at each corner, too wide.

At the bottom of the path sits Bethan Clothier. Her expression is fearful and she shifts in her seat, fretting. The cart that she sits in creaks menacingly – it is Megan's donkey-cart, in need of oiling and repair, unfit for a burden such as Bethan. In front of her, the black donkey, in his twenties, irascible, not pleased to find himself hitched up to the cart.

Megan was not at home; Bethan could not find her, she shouted Megan, Megan Capity but perhaps she had gone back up to the ridge because there was no response. Bethan was in a hurry, so worried! Duddon had come stumbling down the hill saying Bethan, bring a cart and she had gone to Megan's because she knew it would be the quickest and though Megan had not been there, she had taken the cart just the same. Bethan is afraid that she will not be able to control the donkey once she turns back down the hill – she is still swaying from all that wine – and she is afraid to know just what it is that the men are carrying on their shoulders.

At last, the men arrive. Their faces are red and their arms are breaking under the weight of their burden. They do not speak, not even Reilly and Duddon, who are always chattering. They do not look at Bethan, do not stop to explain but they hurtle towards the cart behind her just as fast as they can and as gently, as carefully as their exhausted arms allow, they drop their bundle into the creaking cart. Bethan clicks to the donkey, grits her teeth, prays to God that she will be able to control the cart as it wends its way back down the hill.

And it is only once the ground is less bumpy and the path more level, the donkey securely under control that Bethan dares to turn round, dares to face what she feared she already knew – that the men had just found, in the shallows of the swanny-pool, the lifeless, rotting body of Donald Capity.

Of all the people, it was only Nathaniel who had noticed that Donald had gone, been gone too long, that this time, this time there was something awry. Every dawn, while the full turmoil of the wedding preparations was under way, while everyone in the valley was up in arms with excitement, while Myfanwy plotted and cooked and brewed, Nathaniel trawled the valleys and the beaches and the forests. He looked under trees and down holes, he turned over stones, he left nowhere, nothing unsearched. He barely slept, searching diligently, lovingly, hopelessly for his friend, his companion, his helpmate who had so abruptly abandoned him.

Were they not so caught up in their golden age, in their grandest of days, the people of the valley would have heard the thump-thump-thump of his seven-league boots. They would have heard the silence that came down from his workshed, they would have heard the change in tone of the Celtic pipes, how the gaiety came to be subsumed by a tragic, plaintive moaning. They would have sensed that something was happening, they would have remembered their old charge, common burden of their guilt. Where is Donald Capity, they would have asked, why is he not here with us today, drinking the wine, eating the food, laughing as we are?

On the dawn of his wedding, Nathaniel is ten miles from the valley. All night he has searched. All night he has called Donald's name, looking for clues, straining for a tiny peep that might indicate where he has gone. Where is he now?

Why has he gone like this? What can have made him run away when for twelve, thirteen years, he has stayed so close? And why now, when the mares are due to foal, first of June, when the weather is good and the grass dances high in the sun?

All night he walks, all day. No echo, no answer and as he makes his way back towards the village scouring the landscape, scanning every bush, every hollow, Nathaniel comes to understand that he cannot do this alone, that he must have some help. Maybe if he asks the villagers, they will find him in time. Maybe they will help to prevent what Nathaniel fears, they will save Donald, he will be able to tell the boy that he loves him still, that he cares for him still, that he is at heart a woodcarver and a stallion-man, that he is always, as he always has been, in need of a patient assistant.

By the time Nathaniel returns to the valley, it is close to dusk. He is too rapt in his anxiety to hear or see or sense anything of the rowdy celebrations and all he knows is that he must find them, that he must ask for their help. He goes to the church but no one is there. He goes to the tavern but it is shut up and silent. He runs to Megan's bothy but there is no sign of life, none at all and he is just about at his wits' end when he hears and he feels the ripples of laughter that have been rocking the valley throughout the day, since early dawn. He walks up the hill, tired, footsore, heavy-hearted. He sees bodies strewn about the place, soaked with wine, stuffed with food, dishevelled, dissolute. He has dirt on his hands and his face, dust in his eyes, dry balls of choke in his throat. He says will you help me find the boy, will you help me find Donald?

Bodies begin to stir. Laughter dies, hands move, feet

163

grope for purchase. Heads, smeared in hair, rise up. Faces, blotchy, spent, look round. Sprawling legs straighten, torsos rise. Now they are up and they rub their cheeks with their hands, trying somehow to make themselves feel less ridiculous than they look. All of a sudden, the humour has drained from the day. The men bark at the women, the women bark at the children, the dogs scuttle back down the hill before they in their turn get kicked. Hot shame washes over them. Donald, they say. Aaah yes, Donald. Hot shame and a slow dawning of guilt.

He says he has been gone ten days now. Ten days, he says. They had not noticed. In their self-absorption, in their excitement over Myfanwy's wedding, they had not noticed. Father Duncan, stricken with sudden dreadful insight, falls to his knees. Megan Capity blanches, spins on her axis, heads off running in the direction of the fell. Shiny Blackford mutters under his breath please Almighty please Almighty ... but he is too slow, his thinking too murky after all that wine and all that food.

Then like a thwarted samaritan presented with the spectacle of a drowning man, Tom Sebley steps forward. Alone of the villagers, Tom Sebley has steered clear of the wine-fountain. Always canny, now Tom can profit. He sees the scene – drunken figures, desperate man-god – and he understands that now, here is his chance. Tom Sebley keeps his cool. He does not jump about or wave his arms or shriek but he steps forward and he takes charge like he used to, all those twenty years ago.

The men split up. Tom Sebley says you go that way, Albert; you that way, Reilly; you over the top, Duddon. He says look hard, boys, he says, look high and look low, he says, find him, he says, find Donald Capity. Tom does not think to talk to Nathaniel, to ask him where he searched and for how long and when did he last see Donald and what did he think had caused it this time. You would think Tom had not seen Nathaniel, the way he just passes over him, the way he just leaves him there standing. But as Tom goes to join the search, you hear him mutter under his breath just you stay where you are, talk to that fancy new wife of yours why don't you?

Perhaps everything would have been different if Nathaniel had found Donald and not Tom Sebley. Perhaps if he had not ignored Nathaniel but said to him you go to the swanny-pool, Tom Sebley would not have had the chance to unleash the resentment harboured within him. Perhaps if Nathaniel had disobeyed Tom Sebley, if he had gone up the winding track through the forest to the sky, he too would have seen the strewn fibres from Donald's red shirt, the shredded matter of his trousers and his hat, his underclothes, his boots as they lined the way up the last few steps to the swanny-pool.

But in the event, it is Tom Sebley who first sees the naked floating body, bumping back and forth against the central rock, covered with bird droppings, with flotsam, with pine needles that have fallen down from the trees above.

At first, Tom does not react. He does not shout out, cry out, he does not wail or rush about, tear down the mountain path as fast as he can to spread the dreadful news. Overwhelmed by sudden, touching grief, Tom Sebley stands still, his hands draped uselessly by his sides. The only sounds are the gentle lapping of the water against the swanny-pool edges. The water glints in its magic diamond way, the corpse bulges up like some unknown antediluvian creature and at

165

last, Tom Sebley falls to his knees, reaches out to the water's edge, draws in by its hair the dreadful, bloated thing. Tears, few and dry, fall into the rose-pink waters and disappear.

For some reason, instincts come as one. Within moments of Tom Sebley's discovery, Albert, Reilly, Duddon, Shiny find their way to the swanny-pool. Next Nathaniel himself appears, too late to help draw the body out of the water, too late to show some private, sudden shock. Already Tom Sebley, Nib, Reilly, Shiny are lifting the body while Duddon is hurtling his way down to summon Bethan Clothier.

Duddon only tells her that they have found something – he tells her to fetch Megan, at once, quickly Bethan, then bring up some kind of cart, not to be slow, run, woman, run. He does not tell her that it is Donald and he does not tell her that he is dead. Bethan cannot find Megan. She looks everywhere, shouts up the path, down in the garden, upstairs in the bothy. The long tussocky grass of Megan's garden reaches out, knotted, to trip up red-cheeked, muzzy-headed Bethan. She is blustering, puffing, chasing after the old donkey, fuming and desperate.

Then they are there, the men are there with their burden. Against the odds, Bethan has made it in time. Burden aboard, she makes her way down the hill, gritting her teeth, bracing her hands against her knees so that the donkey cannot run away with her down the bumpy track. By force of will and fear, she makes the trip, reaches the bottom, drives straight to the church. Still red-faced, gripped with fear, she bangs with all her force upon the great west door until the bosses seem to stare at her like two hundred and thirty-seven glaring eyes.

*　　*　　*

166

The great west door creaks to. Behind it, Father Duncan with that timid, *farouche* look of his. He peers out saying yes? maddeningly slow. He is wheezing. He has run down from the top ridge like a maniac, his head pounding, the food in his belly bouncing up and down like stones. He has barely had time to wipe his face, say a prayer or two because he knows, because the tiny whispers of doubt that were pulsing across his chest seem to have merged into one long, throbbing yell.

Slowly, slowly he opens the door. He sees Bethan. He sees the donkey, the cart. He sees the boy – man now – strapped unceremoniously in the back and at last he crosses himself. Lord save us. Lord have mercy on his soul.

Now the men, slouching down the mountainside, their shoulders drooped, their voices stunned into silence. Tom, Albert, Reilly, Duddon. Shiny, his legs wavering, his heart in his mouth as he ponders how Megan will be when she sees what has happened. Behind them all, Nathaniel Cadwallader who seems destined to be just too slow today, just too far behind.

The people slowly come, all the women and the children, all the farmers and villagers, some of them fresh from the ridge because the party went on all night, it did. They may be drunk or woolly-headed but the news has spread as dreadful news does and faces soon float into doorways, edge to windows, appear in the village square. A low, grave murmur runs throughout the valley.

You see the people, you see inside the church where Father Duncan is dismally anointing the body. You see Nib Penhaligon and Duddon and Reilly in the tavern, their heads in their hands. You see Myfanwy and she is drifting up and down the long ridge, picking up a cup here, a plate there, tossing a flower over her head, a feather, sitting down every now and again to study the drawings that cover the longest of tables. You see Nathaniel Cadwallader sitting alone on the throne on his limestone wedge, birds pecking his boots, stallion grazing in the field below. You see Tom Sebley alone in the woods pulling the petals one by one from daisy after daisy after daisy.

But where is Megan? Why is she not here, in the tavern, at the swanny-pool, in the church, in her bothy? Surely by now she has returned from the fell?

Shiny looked everywhere. Once his thoughts cleared and he saw what they found up by the swanny-pool, Shiny ran all over, through the top paddock, round the high fell. He went to her house, down into her garden, round the graveyard, up and down the pews in case she was just praying or leading her goats or maybe dousing her face in cold water to bring herself back because they were all too drunk, far too drunk. But he cannot find her and he is desperate now and he comes back to the village and sits in her bothy, to wait.

Father Duncan, he tries too to look for her but his legs are heavy and his loins are churning so he turns to prayer, on his knees on the flagstone floor adjacent to the rough-hewn table that bears Megan's dead son and he prays that she will come back soon.

Nathaniel Cadwallader, back in his workshed, chipping away at The Word, waiting like they all are, waiting.

A pall of horror descends over the village – silence, shame, dread because when she does return, it will be awful and they will all be responsible.

Then at last Tom Sebley comes down from where he has been lurking in the woods and he comes to the bothy and he says to Shiny as how they should go and search for her again, as how he doesn't reckon she'll be coming back otherwise and he says we should go separate, does Tom, he says you go up the path to the top forest, Shiny and I'll head past the church towards the fell.

And so once again Tom is the hero of the hour because there she is, standing by one of the stretches of dry-stone wall that reach from here to there across the fell. She stands, though he would not know it, her back to the path, on the very spot where Donald was conceived. She is stock-still, her arms crossed, one hand cupping each of her breasts. On the ground, at her feet, her bulrush hat.

Megan does not know for sure that Donald is dead – but some dismal instinctive voice has brought her here, brought her to return to the scene of that day all those years ago when Donald first came into her life. She does not see Tom Sebley, she does not turn round when he approaches. She is lost in the pain of that day, in the helpless humiliation, in the unchangeable changes that he wrought with his pipe-cleaner legs and the gristle in his trousers. She is lost in the sadness that tells her of all those years she might have had with Shiny Blackford, all that family, all those happy times.

And then she feels an arm being slipped about her and she sinks into it, believing that her Shiny Blackford has found her, that he has come to save her, that he has come to take her as he always said he would.

And he does not tell them, Tom, when he carries her unconscious body back down into the village, into her bothy and they are standing there waiting, he does not tell them how it really was.

How he came up behind her and he slipped his arm around her; how he squeezed, just a tiny squeeze because he was struck with pity for her, longing too because she was so lovely there; how at last she looked round, drawn out of her reverie and saw who it was; how she threw him off with a sickened thrust of her shoulder, panic rising, folded down upon the dried earth of the fell, screamed in a blood-curdling, bone-rattling scream get-off-me, get-off-me, on and on and on; how he stood there, hot and cold, frightened, injured pride, unable to placate her, unable to stop her scream so he shouted it out, shouted Donald's dead, Donald's dead, because it was the only way to make her hear him; how he watched as she cried, as she shook until she had no scream left inside of her, no strength, wearing herself out, pushing herself through to darkness, numbness, lifelessness.

Only he carries her down, triumphant he is because it is he who has found her, hero of the hour; triumphant because he can feel it coming back, his place in the village; and when they look at him, quiz him, he explains it away saying she's taken it bad, taken it right bad.

Many days later and still the village and the valley are stiff with shock. Everyone knows about Donald Capity. Everyone knows that had it not been for Tom Sebley, they might never have found him. Without Tom Sebley, who knows, perhaps Donald would have rotted entirely in the rose-pink waters of the swanny-pool? They might have been none the wiser. Everyone knows too that it was Tom Sebley who found Megan for they were all there and they all saw as he lurched into the shadow of the church, Megan Capity lying limp in his arms, numb and lifeless as she was all those twenty years before.

The nights in the tavern have lost their zest. No longer do those lads, grown men now, the Penhaligons and Duddon Sheepshanks and Reilly MacReilly, chortle and snigger into the depth of their glasses. Bethan Clothier and Bessie Hotblack, whose appetites for gossip and idle chit-chat were insatiable, they find their tongues stilled. Shiny Blackford nurses his girl, Tom Sebley sits and waits, Father Duncan cowers in the dark of his church listening to the whispering voices. They tell him that this is bad, very bad, they torment his nights and dog his days – and the troubled Father busies himself with the trivia and routine of the church, lighting candles, dusting hymn books, fretting about the pew cushions, sitting in his sacristy over the big Bibles, hoping that if he does not listen, the voices will go away, the words will have no meaning, hoping that if he does not listen, he will not have to act.

Now no longer do the families take their picnics to the field that surrounded the five-mile hedge, no longer do the birds seem to fly upon their backs or the winds blow across the hills like gentle, tender melodies. Now the village, the valley turns in on itself, closes its doors, draws its curtains, turns its face to the wall, stuffs its fist into its mouths, its many mouths and lets out long, low moans which we hear through the winds, through the wailing Celtic pipes, through the crying laments that blow out across the fells.

No one thinks, even once, of Nathaniel Cadwallader. No one steps, even once, up the bumpy track to the octagonal hill to share the grief, the shock, the mourning with the one man who did more for the boy than any other.

*   *   *

For a week after he is found, Donald Capity lies in the church while a silent, morbid line of villagers files past his body, drops a few flowers, a few leaves and petals on his dead man's chest.

Two

They are waiting for the start of the funeral now, waiting to lay him in God's earth. They are waiting until they can say goodbye for once and all, until they can close that cupboard, say aye and it was a damn shame and know that the grief has been spent, that the mourning is safe in the past. They are waiting to see Megan cry, to hear her scream with final grief, to know that she is grieving so that they need not. They are waiting until Father Duncan stands over Donald's form and says the words that will let them all off, relieve them of their burden of guilt for ever.

Nib and Reilly and Duddon and Shiny carry the coffin from the church into the graveyard, into the hole that has been dug close to Megan's bothy. All the women, all the children, all the men stand in rows about the grave. Father Duncan says his words in a long, slow monotone.

No one speaks, no one cries. Megan Capity, at the front of them all but she is mute now, shocked into silence though no one can guess it by jolted memory, and she is only there because Shiny has lifted her there, gritted his teeth and carried her, whispered there we go, my love, there we go.

Old Man Penhaligon there also, wheeled to the graveside by Nib, who does not know, cannot realise what he does.

173

Old Man Penhaligon, as numb and lifeless as Megan Capity and there is an awful parallel as they both stare ahead, their son lying in the dirt beneath their twin, unfeeling feet.

It is a ceremony that is conducted hastily, as though it soiled those who attended. There is no attempt to dwell on the beauty of the passing man. Father Duncan is afraid, his voices growing louder. Shiny Blackford is afraid also, afraid he is going to lose her for good this time. The others, all the Clothiers and Hotblacks, the Joneses, the Jessops are afraid because they know, deep down in some unconscious way, they feel sure that they are to blame, that they could have done something to prevent this. Somehow they should have known, before Nathaniel had to tell them so, that he had gone. Somehow they should have seen, before it was too late, the possible consequences of the marriage. It is a guilt they do not want. The guilt of his conception, the guilt of the bad that has been done not once now but twice to Megan Capity, the guilt of the wedding with all of its abandon, all of its abject dissolution.

People turn, old men turn, young women, all the people, sad faces turn to leave Donald Capity alone in his grave. Shiny carries Megan, Nib wheels the Old Man, Father Duncan clutches the Good Book, rushes hurriedly back to the sacristy. Tom Sebley, who has stood at the front, he too goes to leave when he sees at the back of them all, her face swathed in veils, Myfanwy of Morland. He has not seen her since the wedding – he has not heard one word of condolence or sorrow from her. Where has she been all this time?

No one understands about Myfanwy. They apply to her the rules that they would apply to themselves, assume she is a wife now, assume as they assumed on the day that this was a straightforward marriage, that she loved him, she would be loyal to him and you would see them together, Myfanwy of Morland and Nathaniel Cadwallader. All along, they have ignored the evidence of their own eyes – that she is just a child, that she takes men as lightly as she might take bread or milk, that at the feast and even during the preparations, he was nowhere in sight. They have feared her as a real threat to him, to them, to the valley. Perhaps it was Donald himself who misled them at first, who misinterpreted what there was to see between Myfanwy and Nathaniel Cadwallader. Or perhaps it was only that Donald feared what they all would fear, that he was one of them after all and did as they would do.

And because they do not understand about Myfanwy of Morland – because they do not see that all she is is a selfish, vain, scheming child who has even now fallen out of her infatuation for Nathaniel – and because they do not understand that the wedding was a farce, they see it all wrongly and they react in all the wrong ways. Do they really believe that Nathaniel was complicit in her schemes – when they know from their own eyes that he was not? Do they really believe that Nathaniel wishes to leave them – when it was he after all who searched for the body? Do they imagine that he does not care about Donald's death, that all those years with Donald, all those years when he made him smile mean nothing?

Since Donald's death, Tom Sebley has been burning inside. He has lost his confessor, he has lost the one person since Father Standage to whom he could be close. He was humiliated, more than he could bear, by Megan Capity's rejection of his sympathy on the fell. He had meant it as kindness, as a simple act of simple kindness and all it seems

175

to have done is to send her spiralling into apoplexy. He does not understand why, not really and he is insulted by her rejection, afraid of her pain, unbearably sad for his loss.

He seeks to blame. He is angry with Father Duncan, that he came at all when he was clearly not a patch on his predecessor. He resents the fact that Myfanwy does not honour him with the glances she bestows on the others. He hated the great feast on the top ridge, how grand it was, how he did not feel a part of it. He hated the game with the tablecloths and he wishes that he could go back now, erase his drawing for it was far too good, far too poignant for her. He had never meant Nathaniel Cadwallader to become the hero in this valley – this was Tom's valley, his valley, my village. They were his people and, but for a pair of meddling out-comers who entered into their midst in a cloud of hocus-pocus and turned everyone's heads, it could have been all right, it could have stayed the same. How dare he? How dare she?

So many things, so many sad and bad things. There is a swirling nausea, makes him feel giddy, makes his wrists prickle and his forehead, makes his vision come and go and he turns in this fragile, fevered state and he sees Myfanwy of Morland, the cause of all this and he hisses you! You! Then he rolls a poisoned dart of spit on his tongue and hurls it as you would hurl a missile and it lands plumb square in her eye.

They all see it. They see Tom with his lips creased up around his eyes and that taut feeling about him, the bubbling aggression. They all see her as she brings her wrist to her eye to wipe out his saliva. Everyone who witnesses this gesture recoils from it. It is ugly, it demeans them all and it is too bare-faced which is not how they would like to be, not at all. Bessie Hotblack cannot get over it, she says later to Mary Jessop who had been too far on the other side of the churchyard to see, cannot understand what can have come over Tom Sebley that he would do such a thing. Reilly and Duddon and Nib, they too are amazed and at least a little ashamed of Tom Sebley's attack. Only Myfanwy, only she remains unmoved, stands as she walks as she lives, apparently oblivious, apparently unstirred by this painless and yet oh so violent of attacks.

But the voices inside Father Duncan, they know. They know that Tom Sebley has said for the first time what they will all come to think. They know that one way or another Myfanwy of Morland and then Nathaniel Cadwallader are the ones who are going to bear the brunt of all their guilt. They know, Father Duncan's voices, they know that this guilt is too great a burden to go unshared, that it must somehow find an outlet. And they know too, Father Duncan and his voices know that he should act, that for once in his life he should use all that faith, all those years of learning in that wretched love-forsaken seminary, all those parables, all God's precious words to stop Tom Sebley, to save the village from its folly, to save all those Clothiers and Joneses, Jessops and Penhaligons from causing themselves, their life, their valley, an even greater, even more irreparable harm.

His funeral made no difference. To a man, they had hoped that it would. Somehow, they hoped, it would help to dispel the grief, relieve the gnaw. Perhaps at last a twenty-year-long episode had come to an end. But days turned into weeks and it did not seem to be so.

Father Duncan became more and more troubled by his voices. They whispered to him as they did when he was a child, when he was a student, as they did in the early days before he found his faith. They crippled him into some awful form of inertia and he knew, if he dared to face it, that this was what he was made of, that after all he was not a leader but a follower, not a saviour but hopeless, spineless.

The swirling nausea within Tom Sebley did not seem to ease, only it worsened because twenty years is a long time to wait in the shadows, because too many wrongs had been done to a resentful man. So he did not let time heal his grief or his shame but he mulled it all over and over, turning it round, changing it until it made sense to him, until it justified his pain. At last, he came to see that that day on the top ridge when Nathaniel had come and told them all that Donald had disappeared, he had all but accused them. He had all but said they should have noticed, they should not have been drunk, they should have put down their glasses and searched. He came to see, Tom Sebley, not that Megan had dissolved in fear from his embrace but that she had turned and spat in his face, that she had slapped him, that she had brought down a thousand insults on his name. He went over and over those last minutes in Donald's life, those last minutes up at the swanny-pool and it seemed to him, after a while, that it could not have been so, that Donald could not have meant to do it, that indeed he had fought and struggled against someone, something, that his head was all but held down underwater.

In sharp succession, two events took place which added to the valley's air of siege. Megan's goat Daisy succumbed to the rigours of old age and tumbled down a rift on the lower fell – stone-dead she was, and the rift was so narrow and so deep that Shiny, for all his efforts, was unable to reach the body and retrieve it for burial as he felt he surely must.

Next the turn of Old Man Penhaligon. For years, the soundless, motionless version of the Old Man, head lolling in his lopsided, giant-wheeled, cart-chair had been a familiar sight around the valley. Then one day, early in the morning, Nib was pushing his father up the bumpy track, going for a stroll. He had no goal in mind, was just enjoying the morning air, letting some of it blow softly over his father's still and shrivelling bones. Suddenly, the chair bumped against a large stone. It lurched forward and the Old Man was propelled out and downwards so that his head banged upon the ground. Nib reached into his pocket, pulled out a cloth to wipe away the spot of blood that appeared from the Old Man's nostril. He thought no more of it, set him up again in the chair and turned round to walk back down to their cobbled yard.

The day was sunny. From cool early morning breezes, now there was a light haze and the sun was beaming through and Nib, as he had done all these past years, parked the Old Man in the warmth. So it was not until the end of the day when Nib was ready to spoon through the Old Man's cracking lips the gruel which was all he could eat now, that Nib noticed an unusual frozenness about him. Nib spoke a few words but there was no hint of comprehension. He shook him but there was no response. He ran as fast as he could to the church and he called Father Duncan, Father Duncan and he said quick, Father, come quick, the Old Man is going.

He was going sure enough, for when Father Duncan came, he found him dead, cold dead, his chin at long, long last free of that never-ending trail of spittle.

They buried the Old Man in the churchyard. Nothing fancy, no stone, just a crooked wooden cross made by Nib and, in a bottle by the cross, a handful of foxgloves and some honesty.

Day after day, Nib came to kneel by the grave of his dead father. Tears sprang up in the corners of his eyes. He was horrified and frightened by the Old Man's death. What should he do now that the dribbling, lolling-headed creature no longer needed him? How would he go on, a ruby among rocks? Nib had no courage. He was driven only by the guilt of the sinned-against. His father might have beaten him, humiliated him, broken his spirit, his skin, his bones but Nib missed him so that his days were the same as his nights, one long unbroken void of grief.

Nib turned the Old Man's room into a shrine. Pride of place was given to the cart-chair and to the blanket which had supported his lolling head. Everything that had formed a part of his life was kept polished, displayed, everything down to his hoof-trimmers, everything down to his bendy iron pipe.

And indeed Nib's grief was almost unbearable to witness. It was shameful, shocking almost. To see him cry like that, to see him weep on his grave, to see him bent double with all the feelings and all the gut drained out of him; to see him beg because that is what he did, beg the Lord that his father be allowed entry to the eternal paradise; to see him push about the cart-chair, empty, and there, in the deep of his girl-sensitive eyes, all you could read was loss – it made you want to join him, said Bessie, it made you want to weep for him.

One day, prostrate, sobbing, Nib's fingers find in the depths of his pocket the talisman that had been given to him by Nathaniel Cadwallader. Now more than ever he needs the comfort and he squeezes the talisman to feel the solace that this magic piece of cedar has always brought him in the past.

But inside Nib's head, besides the moans of grief, there replays the ugly scene that took place at Donald's funeral. Nib hears Tom's hissed rebuke. He hears the whistle as Tom's spit sails through the air towards Myfanwy's eye and the gasps and the *pther* noise as it lands. He hears Tom's contempt, he sees Tom's eyes and the disgust and the loss of faith because maybe now Nathaniel Cadwallader is not what he seems, is not as magic as the villagers would like to believe. So, for all that he squeezes his talisman, for all that Nib wants to feel the comfort that the precious woodcarving had previously offered him, a doubt creeps in, a terrible preying doubt.

In all honest truth, Tom Sebley does not sit down and create a scheme which will cause Nathaniel's downfall. But somehow, after all this time, after all this waiting, he must find a way of venting his frustrations.

From just a few silent prayers in the church, a few bad thoughts, a few little things uttered here, uttered there, murmured now to Father Duncan, then to Mary Jessop or to Bethan Clothier, he creates an atmosphere of doubt. He makes light jokes. People say Nathaniel this, Nathaniel that and Tom Sebley says ah yes, that's all very well ... He whispers into the depths of his glass just one or two things – after all, who said he was a god, who said he could do godlike magic – then follows up his whispers with poignant silence so that the words must sink in and make their mark.

Gradually, Tom finds himself becoming braver. One day, he will climb up into the rafters of the church and he will whisper Nathaniel Cadwallader is no more than a man and he blows this whisper out of his mouth so that it rings round and round the roof of the church. Then the people come in and they hear the remnants of this whisper and it drips, slowly it drips into their consciousness.

On another day, he will blow it on the winds, moan it out across the fells and through the valley, so that it is not loud or clear but it is there, all day long – and you might be weeding your vegetables or you might be ploughing in the top meadow or you might be hanging up your washing because today is fine and you are Mary Jessop, always a good housewife, and you will hear these sounds and they will trouble you.

Slowly, slowly the air is being poisoned. Everyone comes to feel threatened. Tom Sebley sows these doubts which the people hear, all the time, on and on. They cannot go to bed but the air rings with them. They cannot climb the hills, walk the forests, work in the fields, brush their hair in front of the mirror, do their washing without Tom Sebley's whispers bedevilling their thoughts. A fear grows, far out of proportion to the situation in which they find themselves, and it comes upon them like a creeping cloud and they do not know how to keep this fear at bay. What will happen next? they ask themselves. And they allow their nights in the tavern, their silent conversations to be haunted with thoughts of crops being destroyed, trees hacked to bits, animals mysteriously let loose so that they drown in the river or the sea.

One day Tom is in the top woods and he wanders through a

clearing, through a cornfield and he comes across the place where Myfanwy first sowed her flowers. Tom has never seen this before. He does not know what the field, the flowers are all about, what she does here or why, but he sees her and his interest is piqued.

Myfanwy's field is no longer the glittering kaleidoscope it was on the day Nathaniel came – the flowers have reseeded sure enough but the place is a sorry mess – dead stalks and new growth, the drooping and dried out mixed in with young blooms that are stunted – yet Myfanwy does not seem to notice her surroundings. She does not hear Tom or see him but she is walking in wavy lines, her hands casually brushing against the stems. Then she comes to a halt, a dreaming stop and she sighs, hums and sighs and you would not know what she was thinking, good, bad, joyous, sad for her back is turned. Tom seizes his chance. Quicksilver, wolf on his prey, he walks towards her and soon his shadow swallows hers. Slowly Myfanwy turns and she sees who it is and she gasps a little because, to give her her due, she has always sensed danger with Tom Sebley.

Tom sees the girl draw back. He sees her golden-green eyes widen and he watches as her breasts rise and fall just a little faster, just a little more perturbed. Tom says why, what have we here then and she might almost be frightened but then he says – whispers – hello my pretty and he watches as the breaths slow down, as she goes soft, woman-soft. Tom puts his hand upon her shoulder and he pulls her woman-mouth up to his. Tom is rough and he is hurried, cruel. He does not say sweet words. He does not stroke her hair or talk into her eyes and soon he is up, tidying his shirt, wiping a small smile from his lips.

Later that evening, while Myfanwy nurses her wounded

pride, returns to the cottage, sees her father in the last throes of death, cries out in horror and pain and self-pity because she has never had to submit before, not like that, Tom Sebley goes into the tavern. He says I have something to say and all the eyes turn because now they have regard for Tom, now once again they see his worth. And Tom says, only this time he does not whisper but he blurts it out, she did it to me, you know, she came and forced herself on me.

And their reaction is one he could only have dreamt of – for they are appalled, chins drop, a shocked silence sweeps over them. How could she? Who does she think she is, a stranger, attacking Tom Sebley like that? And her a married woman . . .

And the night wears on and they cannot let this go for it is too shocking, too riveting and soon, by dint of association, the name of Nathaniel Cadwallader is brought into the debate. They tar him with her brush and as the level in their glasses drops and still the conversation revolves around this scandalous revelation, it comes to be he, Nathaniel, who bears the brunt of their calumny.

Later on again – now it is almost dawn – Nib Penhaligon chances to mention something about his talisman. He says he thinks it has faded, words all slurred because that is how long they have all been sitting there drinking, arguing and they all hear this and they go home, heads filled with beer and murky thoughts.

The next day in church, Father Duncan comes to talk about the greatness of God, about how he looks over us all, protects us all, works for and cares for and loves us all and someone, no one is quite sure who, blurts out better than Nathaniel Cadwallader, more than he does for us now.

In the vestibule afterwards, Bethan Clothier goes up to

Nib and she shows him her talisman and sure enough, neither of them can see nor understand the symbol that the carving once represented so clearly.

Then the Hotblacks and the Penhaligon brothers, then Mary Jessop, then a few of the others produce theirs and they see that they have all faded – where once they could see, now they are blind. Where once they saw a treasure in the palm of their hands, a glinting magic treasure, now they see just a lump of dead, old wood, a lump of dead old wood.

Three

B ut while the tension grows, while the valley rhythms alter and the winds blow with sombre, moody threnodies, deep inside her bothy Megan remains unchanged. Since that day when Tom Sebley found her, she has sat in her wooden rocker. Sometimes, the light from the parlour window catches her dress, dances on the flowers, glows on a section of her shin. Sometimes, the wind blows so hard that the draught which seeps through her doorjamb lifts the hair on her forehead. But mostly the scene is kept in shadow, by the sweeping purple boughs, by the tall dark church.

In the quiet of her parlour, Shiny also sits. Watches as her long fingers rest motionless on the smooth wooden arm, as her eyelids do not flicker but lie flat still against her brows. He watches her lips, they too free of expression, and he dreams of a day when he might see them dance, might see them bright ruby-red, embracing a smile, blurting out a long ribbon of words that will say to Shiny she is back, she is happy, she is his.

From time to time, Shiny leaves the bothy. He needs to move, needs to breathe some air and blow away all that waiting. Once he goes into the tavern – it is a month, maybe two since he was last there – but he is shocked by the atmosphere, so much so that he cannot stay.

On another occasion, he finds himself wandering out of the village towards the bumpy track and the five-mile hedge. Absent-mindedly, Shiny climbs the hill. He has not thought about what he is doing but soon he finds himself on the small granite plateau next to Nathaniel's throne. Shiny has never been up close to the throne before and he examines it with awe. Such detail, such exquisite workmanship!

Round and about, the pyramid of wood, the motley collection of sheds that house Dungarry and sometimes the mares and foals. Down the back, a large flapping tarpaulin and Shiny is not sure what it is, not at first so he goes and he looks and he sees the drawing that they did, the tablecloth panorama of the village and the valley, of Dungarry and the wedding and all that they knew and Shiny realises that it must have blown down from the top ridge only to land in Nathaniel's paddock.

Shiny peers around. He goes into the sheds, round the pyramid of wood, then comes to the chapel. The door is open! Shiny walks into the light that pours in through the doorway. He is surprised to see that Nathaniel is there and goes to step back, take his shadow out of Nathaniel's light – but Nathaniel does not look up, too intent on the final details of The Word.

Shiny watches Nathaniel as he works. It is as though he has not heard him, does not even realise that his sunlight is blocked. Outside, there is a *ppwwerr* as a horse blows a fly off its lips. The tails flick and the sun beams down. Up here, all is as it always has been. Up here, the winds breathe and the grass blows and the view is ever changing, ever the same.

Shiny stands in Nathaniel's light for he knows not how

long. He is captivated by the detail and the effort, by the fineness of the work and yet the panache. He sees an artist. He sees a man who is driven above all to complete his work, above all to do the thing that comes most compellingly.

A thought suddenly comes to disturb Shiny's absorption. Where among all this is Myfanwy of Morland? Where is this great love who came and swept up Nathaniel Cadwallader, drew him up to the top ridge, married him in front of all of them? Shiny looks around this shed, the others, but he sees no sign of her. Surely there would be a veil here, a ribbon there? Surely he would catch a whiff of her catminty scent? Shiny leaves the hill, puzzled, climbs further through the forest, finds the field of flowers. There is no sign of her, no sign at all, flowers everywhere, the dead and the fresh, the brown and then all the colours – only in the middle of all those stalks and all those drooping heads, the impression of a woman's shape, stalks crushed where she had lain and been pressed into the ground by Tom Sebley.

Slowly a thought dawns on Shiny. Was Nathaniel after all not there at the wedding? Was it after all a hoax, a great idiotic hoax and they had fallen for it and they were all angry with the wrong person? Had she realised perhaps in the wake of the feast, in the terrible earth-bumping aftermath of its excitement, that she did not really want Nathaniel Cadwallader? Had she used him simply as an agent for her feast, an agent for her grand dress and her grand party, an object upon whom she could bestow her latest, wildest fancies? Had she left already, gone already, wrought her havoc and run away because that's what girls like her do, they take what they can and then they move on?

Yet the Nathaniel that Shiny saw did not seem to be

disturbed by Myfanwy's absence. From the patience of his art, from the silent concentration which he was investing into The Word, Shiny might have guessed that Nathaniel had not cared for the girl. So Nathaniel was not there at the wedding because he did not love her! He was not there because she was the one, *she* who wished to be loved! Because she did not wish to share her wedding or her lime-light. Because it was her dress and her plan and somehow she would not allow them to be eclipsed.

And Shiny, who is closest to the truth at this moment, is still not there. For not even Shiny, who is a good man, who has decency and kindness in his veins, can bring himself to see, even here, even now when he is up close to him, sharing the air that he breathes and the light that he works by, that Nathaniel is just a man, no more than a woodcarver. And more than that, that inside of him there is a beating broken heart.

If he could only see inside, he would see how Nathaniel is wounded, weeping. Inside there is the gnaw of his pain for his lost friend Donald. And inside too there is the gnaw of the pain that she caused him. Donald was right! After all, he was right – and nobody guessed, they all thought it was about her, they did not know, only Donald knew and maybe Tom Sebley, that it was about him too, about Nathaniel too, that he did not want her any more than they did, that she made him love her, that she turned his heart and his head, that she took him and she wrung him out, that she fell for him and she taunted him and when at last he gave in to her, she dropped him – like you might drop a leaf or a flower, dropped him down.

Oh yes, my God, he had loved her. My God, he had taken all those dreams to his bed of her eyes, of her hair, of the way she spoke and the way she did not, of the way she drifted in, out of his light, of the way she had barred his path or found herself in his fields, of the way she sowed all those flowers and knew, just knew that that, above all, would bewitch him.

He had loved her but he stayed calm, on the outside, calm because he did not, could not afford to love, because his art was it all, his work, and besides that everything else must wait; because now he was absorbed in The Word and he must finish it before he could think of beginning to love her, marry her or leave as she had begged him, leave. He had not known about the wedding because she did not tell him so he was not there and he never would have been, it was all too soon, there was no time, he must not stop his work, not yet.

And then she had said, on the day before the wedding as it turned out, she had said by the way, I told Donald he could go. I told him I thought it would be better if he went. It had been like a knife driving hot through his heart, the way in which she had said it, so cool, so lacking in comprehension. Suddenly, God seemed to lift, if only for one second, the veil of loving from his eyes. Nathaniel had almost wept with fear. He had gone down upon his knees at her beauteous feet and begged her to tell him, if only she could just God knows remember, in which direction Donald had walked. He had banged his head upon the dirt, his hands, he had said to her in the bottom of his voice, he had said you will never know what you have done, you will never know.

Today, here, now, though he works to the exclusion of all else, though Shiny might not be able to see it because he does not know this man, today, here, now, Nathaniel is like a lion with a huge splinter in his paw. He is bruised and wounded. Nathaniel does not sleep. Nathaniel does not smile. Nathaniel sits upon his throne and now the view that once so entranced him holds only hurt and grief. Nathaniel does not see Shiny standing in his light, Nathaniel is driven to finish these last works because he needs to leave this place where a girl whom he had not sought out, whom he had not even wanted, sought him, took him, was so unwontedly cruel to him and his.

He had come here to be alone, to be with his horse, his dreams, his art. He had happened on the place, he had seen the view and the fells and the knife-sharp hills and he had thought that this was a place kissed by God, painted by God and here on the hill in the chapel he could work undisturbed, dream untroubled. He had come not with a plan but on a whim, not to find love but to find somewhere to call his home, somewhere to root his work. He had wanted some good land for his horse, some good forest where he could find the timber he needed to create his icons, carve out all those things that needed to be said, that his fingers needed to give. That day on the fell, when he had seen her and he had seen the Old Man and all that went on, when he had picked her up and carried her down into the shearing shed, somehow that had sealed it, that had brought him here, that had made him stay.

He had had a friend here, Donald was his friend. Together they had walked a little, ridden, worked with the mares, wandered the length and breadth of the forest. Together, without words, they had had long conversations about the good things, the real things – about the warmth of a horse's breath or the kiss of God's wind or the endless brilliant patterns that form upon the feathers of a barn owl or the smell that comes from the logs on a cold evening when you light them and they are burning well, warming your feet. It had been good to see the boy as he emerged, slowly-slightly from his shell, as he found some things that he really could do, some small way in which his talents could be unlocked.

It had meant more, all of that, much more than any moments trapped in the gaze of Myfanwy of Morland. How blind could he have been! How cruel could he have been to let her do what she had done, to let him think, Donald think, that anything could possibly mean more to him than his art, the horses, their friendship!

Nathaniel Cadwallader, though they might not see it, is just a man and his heart is broken and his illusions are shattered and now, in the place of beauty, he sees cold. He wants to leave, he needs to leave.

Four

By this time almost every mare in this valley and the ones adjoining has been covered by Dungarry. How many years has he been here, this equine god – fifteen, twenty, fifty? It is hard to remember as it is hard to know just how old the great stallion is. Were you to ask him, Nathaniel himself would not be able to say.

Throughout his reign, there have been many crops of foals that have been sired by the great, the inestimable Dungarry. Every foal has been a fine specimen, has more than justified the hope, the expectations of its breeder. All the men who have bought them, worked them, ridden them, have thrilled at the joy that these horses carry in their very bones. Their limbs are sound, their hearts are good, they show the courage of lions. A horse sired by Dungarry becomes a treasured beast and all the breeders rejoice in his name and they send the same mares back to visit him, year on year on year.

Today, in fact, you could almost say that all the horses in this valley and the valleys around have been sired by Dungarry. By now, many of the mares are improbably old. Each year, it becomes a greater struggle for them to bear their foals as they did – but the breeders are superstitious and they prefer to breed every year, year on year on year, from the same mare, same stallion. That way, they know, they can be sure that the stock will be good, that they can take them to be sold at the spring fair and there will be queues of buyers, queues.

In his heart of hearts, every horse-breeder knows that his mare is too old to breed another. He knows that he should go to the market and buy himself another mare to put to Dungarry. How can she bear the weight again on those legs now so galled and stiff? How can she be put through that same cycle of exhaustion and weight and drain when by now she has had ten, twelve foals and they have all been big and they have all taken their share of her?

Nathaniel, too, he should have known better. He should have told them all, last year, he should have said I am sorry, he should have turned them away and spared those older mares. But then, everything was not the same. By then, Myfanwy of Morland was here blinding him with her look, dazzling him with her golden-green eyes. Nathaniel was preoccupied. He did not think to say as he should have, bring me a younger mare but he passed them once more beneath his old friend Dungarry.

Not only that but any doubts that he might have voiced were quickly swept away by the horse-breeders. For some reason, during this year of all years, eloquence and persuasiveness had come to these horse-breeders and every one of them convinced Nathaniel that they should present their mare to the great Dungarry, old and tired and splay-backed though she might be.

So now, eleven weary months on, we are waiting, the horse-breeders, the villagers and farmers, for the new generation. All the mares are heavy, ground-heavy, and

196

their bags are filled with milk and they struggle to lift their feet from the ground, to step from one blade of grass to another. These foals, this year, are sure to be Dungarry's very best. They are sure to be his finest. Why else would the mares be so heavy, so much more expectant than ever before, they ask.

Archie Jessop's is the first to foal. It comes in the night but Archie has been expecting it and he waits up with a candle. Archie, on reflection, does not know why he did not go off to the market and buy himself a new mare. His old mare, her head hanging, no longer seems to relish the only job she knows. Why had he not bowed to common sense and let the old girl rest at last? Why had he not bought that mare at the last fair, the chestnut which had so taken his fancy? Why was it, he wonders? Had there been something, a whisper on the wind, a dream that came to him, a note that was left under his pillow? Or was it just plain old laziness, greed, reluctance to change what had always been successful?

Whatever it was, it had told Archie that to buy a new mare this year would be to do wrong, to risk everything. It had told him that to breed one last time from his old mare would be to ensure his finest, greatest foal ever. Never mind that the old mare could barely stand. Never mind that she had done great service, earned her rest. So the whisper, we do not know how, comes to Archie Jessop. So the whisper persuades an old and knowledgeable horse-breeder to ignore the experience of a lifetime.

Archie Jessop sits with his candle and waits. So excited, he is barely able to sit still. The night is long. He falls asleep, does not hear the mare get down, though God knows he was close enough to hear a pin drop. And he must not have heard her groan with pain nor thrash about nor lie

197

back exhausted, because she was too old, because there was never a foal, because she had succumbed to age and colic and a twisted gut, because Nature or God had intervened and said it is time for her to leave.

The lines that are graven into the contours of his face from a hundred years of squinting into the sun suddenly disappear. Archie Jessop looks into the box and sees the mare, still, barely alive. Every muscle tautens. His face blanches with shock. There is a gulp in his throat. For some reason, he cannot see what there is to see. For some reason, Archie Jessop cannot accept that the mare has died because she was old but he sees that there is a kind of conspiracy, that a curse has been brought down upon him. God help us all, he whispers. God help us all, Tom Sebley was right. Archie Jessop kneels down and prays to the Good Lord for the strength to find and use his gun.

The boys Penhaligon, they too have a mare and she too is due to deliver the same night and it is the same with theirs. She is too old, there was no foal, they could not see that it was greed and not bad luck that brought this tragedy upon them. Soon the word sounds throughout the valley – a plague has been brought upon the mares this year, a plague has been brought on the mares. It is terrible, unheard of. Everyone rushes about, gasping, talking – ignoring all the healthy foals, forgetting all the other, surviving mares, ignoring what they have known for some weeks, that there is some ragwort in the hay, deadly, colic-inducing ragwort. Common sense abandons them to a man. Instead of burning the hay, burying the mares, accepting the rotten luck of it, they stand around in common, stupid horror. No one is there to curb their fears, to tell them that they are being foolish, to tell them that the signs had been there all along if only they had looked. Panic, idiocy, unfulfilled greed take over Archie Jessop, the boys Penhaligon, the valley. Who would have thought it? Tom Sebley was right, he was right! Mothers rush off and place their hands over their children's ears while the crack of the Penhaligon shotgun rings throughout the valley.

Nathaniel Cadwallader, working in his chapel, hears the sound of the gun. It temporarily disturbs him – what can be happening down in the village? – but such is his drive to complete The Word that he soon forgets, pushes the echo out of his head, resumes his fevered chip-chip-chipping.

Father Duncan, who is praying at his altar, he too wonders what has happened – but the whispering voice that plagues him now almost daily tells him to stay where he is, to keep to his praying, to ignore the noise, to assume that bad news will find him soon enough.

Martha of Morland, she hears – but she is packing to leave now because Isaac is dead, because now she has no one and she does not like it here, they are too cold and, besides, she never liked the countryside, never did.

Shiny Blackford does not hear the ringing of the gun for he is deep inside Megan's bothy, trying to raise her from her stupor, trying to talk her back to life so that he can tell her how much he loves her, tell her how much he misses all those years.

But Tom Sebley does, he hears the noise. He sits on his own in the dark of his bothy and a small dry smile comes to his lips.

Later that morning, with the tide of panic swelling in their veins, they call a meeting. They are in the tavern, sitting round, voices hushed, that strange sound of urgency and cluck-cluck-clucking unmistakeable if you walk in, like passing your knife through stones. Archie Jessop says, and they all agree, nod their heads, he says this thing's got to stop. He says, and they all agree again, time's we took things into our own hands, time's we did something, time's we stopped all this.

Tom Sebley sits at the back and he says nothing.

An hour later, they all meet again – this time in the market square, under the shadow of the church, in the view of the octagonal hill. Archie Jessop stands up on a stone, the boys Penhaligon next to him, and he says what are we going to do about it then, how are we going to stop these things happening? Archie Jessop is not a leader of men. He is just angry and disappointed. All the women and farmers that stand before him look at him nonplussed and they do not come up with any answers. They are blending not into a team of individuals but into a tribe and as such, they are weak and they are stupid and they do not know how to stem the tide of their disbelief.

Now it is the middle of the afternoon and the men are meeting once more. This time Tom Sebley is there again, only now he has stepped to the front of the crowd, unable to resist for a moment longer the temptation to show them the way out of this terrible impasse. Now, at last, he can stand up on the stone, he can shout to them all, he can come to lead the men again, lead the villagers, tell them what they must do.

So now, here it comes. At last he dares to vent all the feelings, all the frustration, all the pain, all that grief, contempt, regret that he has stored up for so long now. Now the death of his friend Father Standage, the loss of his friend Donald, the insult of Nathaniel's presence can

200

be laid to rest. He says that man is not from God! He says that man is just a stranger! He says we did not ask him to come and we did not welcome him among us and he has brought terrible things upon us. He says, and now he must draw himself up as he does so, he says THAT MAN MUST GO!

He says he dazzled us because he was a stranger and he came at a particular time. He tricked us with pieces of wood that he said were magic. He tricked us with a horse that was no better than any other. He said nothing and he did nothing that you or I could not do ourselves. And more, he roars, MORE, he did things that you and I, as true residents of this place, would never do. He made Donald Capity kill himself. Yes, he killed a man whom we loved. He could have saved him, he could have drawn him back from the edge of the swanny-pool, he should have known if he was so magic, if he was from God, he should have known how Donald Capity was in his head and he would have saved him.

Now look at her, and here Tom Sebley turns and points to the tiny bothy in the shadow of the church, look at his mother, Megan, how she suffers because of him, because of Nathaniel Cadwallader. Look at your talismans – are they really the magic tokens he said they were? And those mares, those two good mares, now poisoned and dead, now foalless and dead. He is not our friend, that man. He said he came to help us but he has not done that, says Tom, far from that.

Tom Sebley says these things and a thousand others. The sweet sensation of unburdening his heart is so good, so good and he is flushed as he speaks. The air turns from clear to purple. It fills with wasps and flies, with a million biting creatures. But the people who sit in the square and listen to Tom Sebley's words, they do not see the flies nor hear the wasps, they do not feel the stings. They do not cut out from the words the good from the bad. They do not hear the difference between oratory and invective. They do not heed the warning that good and sensible men would heed. All they hear are the words of a man who knows what he is saying, a man who will give them some succour from all of this, a man who, God willing, will bring them back their golden age.

There is the sound of footsteps, a clearing of a throat. It is Nathaniel Cadwallader. He has come to ask the villagers for some help because Dungarry is ill, he too poisoned by the ragwort hay. It seems he is cast at the base of the hill, cannot get up because his legs are too weak. I cannot get him up alone, Nathaniel says. I need some men to help me get him up. Then, he says, he will be able to lead him up the hill into his wooden shed. There he will give him potions, give him water, nurse him, help him, God willing make him well again.

As one, the faces turn and they see him standing at the back of the square, making his quiet, pleading entreaty. For the first time with clear vision they see Nathaniel Cadwallader. For the first time they look into his eyes. He is a simple man, modest. There is a ruddy glow about him, he has working hands, he has an honest face, he is good – not great, just good; not a god, just a man.

The faces turn and the eyes blink and Nathaniel Cadwallader opens his mouth once again and tells the faces and the eyes that he would like some help, would be grateful for some men to come up the hill, to wrap the ropes around Dungarry's legs so they can get him up, so he can walk the old stallion up the hill from the slopes to the plateau. The air is purple still, filled with all Tom's emotions, all the feelings of all the villagers who have allowed themselves to go this far, to work up to such a fever and Nathaniel, who is shy and unused to talking, struggles to express himself. The faces and the eyes, they return a look to Nathaniel that is unblinking.

No one moves when Nathaniel Cadwallader makes his plea. No one stands up and says why sure, why certainly, Nathaniel, let me come and help you walk your old horse to the plateau. Instead they all just stare – empty, stupid faces staring at a good, a simple man. Nathaniel Cadwallader leaves the square. He does not understand.

A few hours after this and Father Reginald Arthur Duncan hears a hefty banging on the great west door. Father Duncan can barely hear himself speak for the whispering voices which are taunting him so loud, so endless. He goes to the great west door and he pulls it open and he sees in front of him, curled around the oafish insolence of Tom Sebley, he sees all the men from the village, all the Duddons and Reillys, the Nibs and brothers Penhaligon, Archie Jessop, Alfred Hotblack, all of them.

They say he must go, you must help us make him go, you must go and tell him, you saw him first, you must tell him to go. They say Donald has died, those mares have died, Megan is ill and we need him to go, Father Duncan, he is making it all bad.

In shock and fear and an inability to deal with confront-ation, Father Duncan retreats in haste to the depths of his church. Tom Sebley leads the men and they too go down the aisle, following the Father. The great west door bangs back and forth in the breeze while Father Duncan rushes up the steps, falls to his knees at the altar, prays to the Lord for help as the sun glows yellow and blue upon his back. The voices inside Father Reginald Arthur Duncan's head are talking now, whole words, saying you knew it was bad, you knew it was bad.

In the circular pool of light that is cast by the sun as it streams through the large rose window of the church kneels a man, a small man. He is meek, cowed, sacrificial. In the cloak of his bible-black cassock, he is swallowed by shadow, his head buried in his hands, crouching in pity beneath the altar. The man is watched by a crowd of men, by many men who stand and wait.

Father Duncan is afraid. He is trembling and he is praying as hard as he knows how but he cannot seem to feel the feeling, know with any certainty that his Lord, his Lord Almighty with whom he has prayed so well these years past is listening to his prayers. Help me, he whimpers, help me. I need to know what I must do. I need to know. To you I turn as to no other.

Father Duncan can feel the weight of the eyes that are boring into his back. He can feel the wind that is blowing in from the gaping great west door, blowing draughty, saying come on, come on, Come On Man. He hears the voice now inside his head, louder now, louder, louder. It says do as you must, it says do as you will, it says listen to Tom Sebley, it says he is right, he is right, you knew it was bad, you knew it was bad.

Father Duncan stands up and he turns round – he has had no answer from the Lord Almighty. Has he been abandoned by his faith also? It seems to him that he has no choice, that he must do as the villagers ask, go to the south-west of the village, up the bumpy track to the top of the octagonal hill, into the chapel to say to Nathaniel Cadwallader, to say to his face you must go, Nathaniel Cadwallader, you must leave us. This is what he must say, this is what Father Duncan sees that he must do. He is buckling to Tom Sebley's will. He is taking, like a child, the revenge that Tom is visiting on him for his unsatisfactory replacement of Father Standage. Father Duncan feels abandoned by his God but all he is, is afraid – all he is, is superstitious and unable to deal with his fear.

Very well, Father Duncan whispers, very well, to the waiting men. With difficulty, Tom Sebley stifles the small, dark smile that once again springs to his lips. He lets Father Duncan pass and they troop, a crocodile of men, out of the church, through the village square, up the bumpy track, through the five-mile hedge to the top of the octagonal hill that is home to Nathaniel Cadwallader.

Nathaniel is not in his workshed when they arrive. He is not on the plateau. They call out Nathaniel Cadwallader, Nathaniel Cadwallader! They say it gruffly and deeply so that he will know, when he hears it, he will know that they have something important to pass on.

But it matters not how the men say it for Nathaniel Cadwallader can hear nothing, he is down the slopes at the back of the hill sitting with Dungarry, who is ill now, so ill that he is no longer thrashing but still.

The crocodile of men troops from one side of the plateau to the other looking for its prey, looking for Nathaniel Cadwallader until someone shouts he's here, down here and the crocodile snakes back on itself, turns and heads down the slopes to where the man sits beside the prostrate body of his dying horse. Tom Sebley pushes Father Duncan to the front. He says go on, man, go on. Father Duncan her-hems, does not look Nathaniel in the eye but says we think you should go. We believe it's time you should be going. Father Duncan is so frightened as he speaks that he does not look down, does not even see that Dungarry lies at his feet, has no inkling that Nathaniel is kneeling by his old friend who is close to death.

Father Duncan says these words and the voice within his head at once begins to die down, to cease its relentless nagging. Then he turns to leave and as he does so, the sudden overwhelming shame at what he has done is too much to bear and he sets to running, fast as he can, bible-black cassock streaming in his wake. At once, the crocodile of men who have snaked in behind him, who have said nothing but nodded stupidly, oafishly in agreement, they catch the fever of Father Duncan's flight and they too begin to run. It is like tipping the snow off a pitched roof. Were it not so cruel, were it not so damning and painful and lacking in all human pity, it would be laughable.

You see a man who is simple, modest. You see a man who is not great, just good. You see a horse that is lying on the ground, his guts all sucked up in pain, his eye rolling, his flanks bathed in sweat. You see as the man touches the neck of the horse, tries to ease his pain – and the horse just lifting a hind leg, just making some last effort to thrash it away.

And behind them, you see, in the backdrop to this scene of dying, a crowd of men running, hurtling down the hill, hats falling, coats flailing, cruel words hanging behind them like ribbons.

Now it is night and everyone knows what has happened. Everyone – all the women who have heard the story from all the men – feels an enormous sense of unburdening. At last, at last, things will be better again! Tom Sebley was right, he was right!

Then at dawn, they hear a shotgun, the ring of another shotgun.

And though they might like to ignore it, they know. They could picture it because they have been there before, they saw Archie's mare and the Penhaligons' mare so they should know what it is. Nathaniel Cadwallader, standing there on the slopes of his octagonal hill. Watching his old friend struggle and fight with a poison that is tearing his insides to shreds. Putting his hand again on the horse's neck, trying to free him from the demons that are attacking his friend from within. If only they had helped him as he had asked, if only they had taken the ropes and pulled him over, he might have walked the old horse up the hill, he might have saved him.

But now it is too late. Nathaniel Cadwallader must say goodbye to Dungarry. There is no secret so close as that between a horse and his man, so they say. There is no bond so strong as that between a horse and his man, between Nathaniel Cadwallader and his beloved Dungarry. There is no pain so strong as that which rips through a man's heart when he must raise his gun to his horse's head and send him on to a place where he cannot be.

Nathaniel holds his gun up between Dungarry's two golden, bottomless eyes. A thousand times through this long night he has wished that this need not be. A thousand times he has prayed that the villagers might come back, that they might step up the sponging hill after all and lend their strength to save Dungarry.

But now he knows it is too late and he holds up the gun and he pulls the trigger and he watches the blood of his old friend roll down the slopes of the octagonal hill, watches the spirit of his old friend as it jerks out of his body and flies off to God knows where. Nathaniel Cadwallader falls down upon the ground and he cries and he cries and the tears pour out and it seems they might never cease. Tears and blood flow down the octagonal hill, flow down round the bottom, down the lane and into the village square.

It is a pool of shame that gathers in the cobbled square, a pool of shame. Soon it is so large that it spills across the threshold of the great west door – but the dark eyes do not come out of their houses on this day, they do not come down from behind their upstairs windows. They know from the ring of the shotgun that they must not. Even Tom Sebley knows better than to leave the bowels of his cottage.

Father Duncan too, he lurks within. He is terribly afraid, sick with fear. He has done a dreadful thing. He is weak, so weak! How could he have been so weak when, with the Lord on his side, he felt so strong? Father Duncan wishes that he might leave the valley, might be given another church in another place. He wishes to run away from this dreadful episode. He wishes to believe that it was good and better what he did but he knows, in his heart of hearts, he knows.

Later that day, there comes a tapping at the great west door. Father Duncan jumps. Who can it be? What can it be? He is so afraid. He wishes it to go away, he wishes that whoever it may be will leave at once, abandon any thought of coming in. He cowers behind a pillar hoping, praying that whoever it is will not try the door and come in anyway.

The great west door creaks open and into the church walks Nathaniel Cadwallader. He is a man whose spirit is broken. He walks with a step that is laboured, that is pained and slow, enfeebled by grief. He is almost ready now to leave the valley. He has no taste for the place where Dungarry has died, where his friend Donald has died, where his heart was broken in pieces by a fearful witch-maiden. In some strange way, he did not hear the words of Father Duncan up on the hillside. He did not see the hostility that was parcelled up in all those men who snaked along behind the vicar. In many ways, he was too decent to see all of that. He was too kind and simple-hearted to believe that men could join together in such a way to be so cruel. Nathaniel Cadwallader leaves because he will, because he must, because he cannot stay where all his happy memories are turned to ash.

But before he goes, he must deliver to Father Duncan his last talisman. Nathaniel approaches the altar. The light, primrose and periwinkle, dapples his back. He reaches into his pocket and pulls out his most delicate work of art. For one last time, Nathaniel contemplates his effort. He holds it up to the light. He turns it, slowly, between his thumb and forefinger so that he can examine all its facets. And as he does so, the sun bursts through and across a radiant blue-and-yellow rainbow, you can see, for one last time, the magic of the art of Nathaniel Cadwallader.

Five

As it happens, the shot which kills Dungarry is the catalyst that frees Megan Capity from her months of oblivion. For weeks now, she has sat in her bothy, in her oak-dark rocker and she has not seen, not heard, not acknowledged the presence of a single living thing. The death of her son, the seeming advances of Tom Sebley, the terrible remembrance of Donald's conception sent Megan into a long, downward spiral.

But now it is dawn. There is a crack that rings out through the lemon-green valley. It is loud and hollow somehow. Megan sits up in her oak-dark rocker and her eyes open wide. At once, a terrible pain strikes through her heart. At once, Megan understands, knows somehow about everything that has happened. She wails, moans out No, No, a long No that blends in with the baleful sounds of the pipes and is lost on the valley's early morning breezes.

With an almighty effort, Megan Capity lifts herself up from the position in which she has stayed for all of this time and she walks the length of her parlour and she creeps up the steps out of her bothy into the graveyard and she sets to running, running, running as fast as her jelly-legs can carry her. She must find Nathaniel Cadwallader! She must find him. She must find the man who saved her son and her life all those many moons before.

Megan is running and in her pocket she feels her talisman. She slows to a walk because she is tiring now and as she does so, she pulls her talisman out of her pocket – how beautiful it is, how marvellous! It is as strong as ever, as grand as ever, as eloquent and meaningful as anyone could have wished. She must find Nathaniel Cadwallader! She must persuade him to stay. He must not be driven away by Tom Sebley, by the stupid sheepish oafs who follow Tom Sebley, who do as he wishes, who speak as he speaks, who know nothing and understand nothing. She must tell him that it was all her fault, that she never loved him, that had she only been able to forget how he had come, then she might have loved her Donald, then he might not have felt so alone, so unable to connect. She must tell him that what he did was good, that what he was was a good friend to her son, that he showed her how to love Donald though God knows it was hard enough. She must tell him that he was never a god, that they never should have thought he was a god, that he was an artist, that it was his gift that was divine, that they needed him because without that gift they were nothing, just farmers, just a valley with a few sheep and a few fields.

Nathaniel Cadwallader breathes the dreams of God. Nathaniel Cadwallader is a fine man, a good man, a man without whom this valley will come to mean nothing.

Megan is the only one who knows. She is the only one who understands. Megan Capity is the only one in all of the valley who understands just what he is, this Nathaniel Cadwallader. She is the only one who can take him as he is, who can appreciate his otherness and yet not expect more of him than there is to expect. She does not say turn my wine into bread, make my goats into fishes.

Megan Capity knows that Nathaniel Cadwallader's greatest gift to her was his friendship with her simple, unhappy son. Thanks to Nathaniel, Megan was granted a few nights' sleep, a few nights when she could say that she was content in her bed. Thanks to Nathaniel, Megan Capity could allay for a few moments the terrible guilt that she felt for not having fought off more effectively the advances of Old Man Penhaligon. Thanks to Nathaniel Cadwallader, Megan Capity understood that her son was not so bad, that after all his wretched conception was not all to the bad.

She must find Nathaniel Cadwallader! She must find him! She is so tired! On she pushes up the bumpy track. Her legs are barely working, barely able to propel her. I must find Nathaniel, I must find him. And then she is there, up on the plateau. With the little strength she has left, Megan calls his name, calls out Nathaniel Cadwallader. There is an echo and Megan knows that she is too late. The chapel looks empty and the door to Dungarry's shed is banging. Megan looks round, trawls the hilltop, down the front, down the sides, calling out Nathaniel Cadwallader, Nathaniel Cadwallader. And then she comes to the back paddock and she sees the white flapping tarpaulin that had caught Shiny's eye a few weeks before. And she goes to look at it, as he did, to examine it and she sees that it is the drawing that they did, the drawing that they all did on that maddest of days.

Now the sun is going down because that's how long Megan has been looking for him and as it does it gleams red through the linen, carries their pictures down the valley, on to the sides of the houses in the village. You can see Dungarry magnified, coloured red, creeping across the back of the Hotblacks' wall. You can see the sheep and the cattle following on behind, tracing their evening journey down the cobbled marketplace. You can see all the dreams that there were, the shadows of the talismans, the pictures of the finest foals, the images of the golden days. You can see when the harvests were good and the children were strong and the people were happy. You can see Donald and Nathaniel walking side by side behind Dungarry's chariot, wood-gathering. On the backs of the village walls through the sunset-brilliant reflection of their tablecloth panorama, you can see the memories of a golden age.

And if you come there now, if you come with me to the top of the hill – now that the valley is empty, now that the Hotblacks and the Clothiers, the Joneses, the Penhaligons have moved away because here it is no longer as good as it was; now that Isaac has died and Martha is leaving and Nib and Duddon and Reilly have gone off to fight in a war; now that Myfanwy of Morland has married Bertie Hotblack and moved away; now that Shiny has died and it is just Megan, old blind Megan Capity who sits upon her chair and turns it as the sun turns round the valley; and Tom Sebley who hides in his cottage, afraid to step outside, no regrets, only those same old fears that seem never to leave him now; and Father Duncan who dances within the darkness of his church, never seen, never spoken to, obsessively attached to a woodcarving which he will allow no one else to view; now that the houses are empty and the pictures are hanging lopsided upon the barren walls and our footsteps echo like old men's bones – come with me and you will know that Megan Capity was wrong, that Nathaniel Cadwallader does not, did not leave this sainted valley.

Step with me up the sponging hill and you will see in

214

front of you the silhouette of a man. We cannot see his face but we can see that he is tall and strong, a giant of a man. He sits in a wooden throne chair and he surveys, beneath an auburn sky, he surveys the view – the only view that ever is – a panorama of rising-and-falling hills, lemon-Irish-green, a humpy, crisscrossing peachy, soft-bottomed view that spreads and seeps into the sea beyond. He is here in the hills, he is here in the haze that caresses the hedge-tops, he is here in the beauty of God's day. He is here in the colours, in the light, in the dark, in the yellows and the purples. He is here in the breaths that you take, in the rhythm of your joy, in the simple, scented perfection of all that you can see.

But what is this? We are not alone. Something brushes you from behind. You turn to look and you see it is the shadow of a conker-brown stallion.

God breathes his dreams through Nathaniel Cadwallader!